Heidi's Children

Charles Tritten

With a Foreword by the author

Published by
Dell Publishing
a division of
Bantam Doubleday Dell Publishing Group, Inc.
666 Fifth Avenue
New York, New York 10103

ISBN: 0-440-40190-9

RL: 4.9

Reprinted by arrangement with Western Publishing Company, Inc.

Printed in the United States of America

March 1989

10 9 8 7 6 5 4 3 2 1

W

Contents

Foreword

*T*here was a time when story writers could end their tales with the words "and they lived happily ever after," and know that everyone would be blissfully satisfied with such a sweeping conclusion. Grown-ups still are inclined to take the author's word as final. But not the younger readers of our day! "Ever after" in their restless imaginations can cover such a multitude of adventures and trials and happy events!

And so these young readers (may their tribe increase) sit themselves down, take pen in hand and write to the author to find out exactly what did become of everyone, including the goats and the kittens, until the day they died.

If I remember correctly (and authors too often have very bad memories) *Heidi Grows Up*, which I wrote as the sequel to Madame Spyri's much-loved story, *Heidi*, ended with Heidi and Peter's wedding day. They were watching the sun as it sank to rest behind the darkening hills of Dorfli. And, if my memory still does not betray me, Heidi was allowing Peter to have the last word: *"It is a promise," said Peter. "But however many times it may return it will never see a happier day than this."*

I can see now that *Heidi's Children* is finished, that I have made a prevaricator out of Peter. For there were many, many happier days in store for both of them. And it has been a pleasure indeed for me to share those happy days with all of you who have written to me to ask whether Heidi and Peter ever had any little children of their own.

A few days ago the mother of a little girl to whom I had been reading these very pages which you now are about to read asked me a question which I have been turning over thoughtfully in my mind. She asked me whether Johanna Spyri might not disapprove, were she alive, of the liberty I have taken in these later books of interpreting for the children of today what the "happily ever after" may have meant in the life of Heidi.

In the first place, I knew Madame Spyri as well as one human could know another. Every book she wrote was a labour of love for the children she knew so well. Each was written in memory of the little "lost one" who used to ask her to tell him what lay beyond "forever after." I know that she never refused to grant a child's wish as long as she lived.

So I went to my desk and showed the mother some of the hundreds and hundreds of children's letters that have come to me since *Heidi Grows Up* was published. "Truly," said the mother, "Heidi belongs to all those children from all those faraway places. Not just the little Heidi, but the Heidi who grew up to such a fine girlhood, to become such a proud young wife, and such a wise and happy mother."

CHARLES TRITTEN

Chapter 1

Springtime in Dorfli

*D*orfli was still enveloped in a mantle of snow but the baker, returning from Maienfeld in his wagon, reported that down in the valley it was already Spring.

Nowhere was this news received more joyfully than in the old manor house at the end of the crooked village street. Opening one of the large windows which looked towards the valley, Heidi rested her elbows on the sill and gazed out. It might be true that down there flowers were already blooming in the fields; blossoms were on the trees; little rivulets were running through as the snow and ice started to melt. Here she could see nothing of this, but there was Spring in the air. Every breath of it was sweet.

Presently Heidi withdrew, leaving the window open, but in another moment she reappeared at the door wearing stout boots, her head uncovered. The longing could no longer be denied. She must go down the road, into the fields and to the edge of the forest. She must go to meet the Spring. To be sure, she was no longer the little girl of yesterday, but she had kept her gaiety, her passion for nature, her childlike excitement for the changing seasons.

1

Following the road down to Maienfeld, she said to herself, "If only I can meet the Spring, how happy I shall be."

Today she thought of the Spring as a gay messenger-boy and smilingly she imagined him "in a beautiful apple green suit with daisies studding his shoes" as it says in the song.

Just at the turn of the road, where there was a large open place, Heidi saw the first flower, almost hidden in the bank. Ecstasy filled her. It was true. The long winter had passed and with Spring would come one of the greatest joys that a young wife can ever experience. For both Peter and Heidi felt that no marriage was complete until it was blessed with children. Spring held this promise. Even at the wedding the great event had been prepared for and the cradle had stood ready. This was the custom. Often, at a <u>Grisons</u>[1] wedding, the cradle was prepared and a child walked with the bride and groom carrying wheat. This was a sign that the marriage would be fruitful, that there would soon be children. Now Heidi's cherished wish was to come true and, with the first strawberry blossoms, she looked forward to holding her baby in her arms.

Never had she known such joy as surged over her as she beheld the first delicate snowdrops. Anemones, golden colts-foot blossoms, whole fields of crocuses, and strawberry blooms would soon follow and, with Summer, she might be able to close up the great manor house and take her baby up to the chalet on the Alm. There the high slopes would be crimson with glorious Alpine roses and every breath of the refreshing mountain air would be perfumed with fragrance.

It was on the Alm that Heidi had spent the happiest days of her childhood. It was there she had met Peter and neither of

---

[1]The canton (or state) in which Heidi lives.

them could imagine anything better than living there again with children of their own.

Now Heidi looked up to the Alm where the hut was still deep in snow. Light snowflakes were still falling but they melted in the sun before they touched the ground. Yes, Spring was really coming and with every patch of green Heidi beheld the miracle taking place before her eyes.

As the clock in the church steeple struck four, Heidi turned back towards Dorfli. School would be out and, if she hurried, she might meet Jamy, the schoolmistress, and tell her the delightful news of the first Spring flowers.

Children trooped past her on the road and she hailed them with, "Spring is coming! If you look closely, you may see a flower along the roadside."

She reached the schoolhouse just as Jamy was leaving and the two friends walked together as far as the post office where Jamy stopped for her mail.

Jamy, or Jeanne Marie, as she had been christened, was a native of Hungary, but had lived a good part of her life in France and also in Vaud, a French-speaking canton in south-western Switzerland. Heidi had met her at the school near Lausanne where she had been educated. Heidi's godfather, the good doctor from Frankfurt, had sent her there in order that she might take violin lessons and improve her French. But Dorfli was home, and Heidi had returned to teach in the same village school where Jamy now taught, and later to marry her play-mate, Peter the goatherd, and take care of her grandfather who was old and needed her. Shortly after her marriage the <u>doctor</u> had been taken suddenly ill. His <u>last wish h</u>ad been that Heidi should have the house where she and her grandfather had what he liked to call their "winter quarters." The rest of his fortune went to his adopted son, Chel, who was now studying art in Paris.

The doctor's house was large and at first the possession of it had only confused Heidi. The bare floors and the wide halls echoed to her footsteps, and the place seemed peculiarly empty without the doctor. The wind whistled and blew through the cracks in the more remote portions of the house, and whenever she entered these rooms Heidi soon found herself flying back towards her old "winter quarters" which included the kitchen.

Of all the rooms, the kitchen seemed least changed by the death of the doctor. Brigitte, Peter's capable mother, still considered it her kingdom and it was good to find her stirring batter or putting potatoes on to boil just as she used to do. For Brigitte had kept house for the doctor and his adopted son and Jamy had boarded with them. Now she continued to board with Peter and Heidi. Nothing was really changed in the house. Only the kindly spirit of the doctor had gone out of it.

Boarding the schoolmistress was considered a great privilege in Dorfli and, as the manor house was by far the finest in the little hamlet, Heidi was spoken of as "the fortunate godchild." The villagers, having little else to take up their thoughts, often gathered in groups to discuss the past, present and future of the manor house and its occupants. There was such a group around the post office when Jamy came out and joined Heidi, who had been waiting for her at the steps. In Jamy's hand was a letter bearing a French stamp.

"You've heard from your father?" asked one of the more curious villagers. It was well known to all of them that Jamy's father had recently been appointed Hungarian military attaché at Paris. It was also suspected that he did not altogether approve of the position his daughter had accepted as teacher in the little mountain hamlet.

"No," Jamy replied to the question. "This letter isn't from my father. He's much too busy to write."

Then she pulled Heidi along until they had passed the group. Stopping under a beech tree, which was already beginning to show a few leaf buds, she added, "It isn't from Mama either. She never bothers to write. It's from Marta, my little sister."

"Is anything wrong?"

Heidi asked the question anxiously, for she had not forgotten the delicate eight-year-old child who had come to Dorfli for her wedding and stayed on for a time at the Ragatz spa to bathe in the thermal water and grow strong.

"Her health is all right, if that's what you mean. It is something else that is wrong. But here, read it for yourself and you will see."

With that Jamy handed Heidi the letter.

Dear Sister:

We are here in Paris, staying in a big hotel, and I am lonely. Mama told Papa that they could go out and have good times except for me. The nurses leave every time I get sick because I can't help screaming and that scares them. Papa told Mama that I could be put in a Swiss school and if you write maybe they will put me there. Then I can be near you. I won't scream. I promise. And I won't get sick. Could I go to the school you teach? Mama says now you are a peasant and I think I would like that. It would be like the wedding. Please write and say you will take me. Somebody has to want me . . .

And here the page was quite smudged, as though tears had fallen on it. Underneath, the child had simply signed her name. That was all there was to the letter. It was written in French, badly spelled and filled with erasures and smudges, but Heidi could easily read it and the pathetic appeal went straight to her heart.

"Of course she'll stay with us, Jamy. We want her."

"I knew you'd say that," Jamy answered, squeezing Heidi's hand. "But will Peter like it? And what about your grandfather? He is old and the house should be quiet. It's true that Marta does have screaming spells when nothing seems to comfort her. And what will Brigitte think about a strange child coming into the family when you will soon be having a little one of your own?"

"How can that matter?" cried Heidi, her face beaming with happiness. "I've always wanted a little girl to mother, and if this child needs a home, I see no reason why she shouldn't have a home with us. Grandfather is fond of children and Peter's mother dotes on them. She's never quite forgiven Peter for growing up."

Jamy had to laugh at this. Brigitte still called her son Peterli[1] although he was six feet tall and strong and brown as a chestnut.

"She'll be baking little cakes for Marta and knitting mittens when the cold comes again and—oh, Jamy!" exclaimed Heidi, her plans mounting still higher, "we can take her up on the Alm with us this Summer and she can play in the pasture just as I used to do. We're going up as soon as the baby comes and Grandfather is strong again. That's what I love so about the Spring. It's full of promises. Marta can spend every day in the

---

[1]Little Peter

sunshine and by the end of Summer she'll be so well you will hardly know her. I knew something good was about to happen. I felt it in the air the moment I opened the window. You remember how it was with Clara? Why, she even learned to walk because of the high pastures! There isn't anything too good to happen on the Alm."

"If you can give Marta part of your faith in these mountains and the Lord that made them, that will help," said Jamy thoughtfully. "She's so timid. Perhaps you've noticed how she shrinks away from everybody as though she were afraid of being hurt. And she seems to take no pleasure whatsoever in the beautiful scenery around the lake in Vaud. She's been that way ever since Grandma died and she no longer had the loving care she needed."

"She still had her mother."

"I know," Jamy replied sadly. "But Mama is so nervous. I told you how she was when we were in school. She and Marta frighten each other as neither of them can stand the sight of tears. I've tried to be close to her, but we've been separated more than most sisters and I suppose the rest of the family have just about given her up as hopelessly shy and unsociable."

"She didn't appear so at the wedding. She was a little afraid of Grandfather and kept a good distance away from him. But otherwise she seemed quite happy."

"Your grandfather is a rather terrifying person," laughed Jamy, "until you've made his acquaintance. Probably it's only because of his beard and his shaggy eyebrows. I've noticed he has a very pleasant twinkle in his eyes."

"He's a darling," said Heidi warmly. "I do hope the fine weather that's coming cures the pain he's been having in his chest."

Now they approached the house and Heidi could see a thick curl of smoke coming out of the chimney. No doubt Brigitte was already busy preparing supper. She did most of the cooking in the spacious kitchen which served as a dining-room as well. But the house was large and Heidi's own hands found plenty to keep them busy. Everything—tiles, windows, floors and eating utensils—all were spotless. The slate-topped table reflected the face of anyone who stood over it and the white pine, out of which the grandfather himself had carved a great many pieces of furniture, was rubbed until it was as smooth as satin. And what a good, clean odour came from the room! Now, as they swung open the heavy oaken door, the house was filled with another odour—that of caraway—for Brigitte had just emptied the oven and on the table was a whole pan full of little round cakes.

"You must already have guessed what we have to tell you," cried Heidi, running into the kitchen and throwing her arms about the waist of her mother-in-law.

"Indeed! I have guessed nothing," the woman exclaimed. "These cakes are for Peterli. He tells me that Spring has already come in the valley and with Spring comes an appetite for cakes."

The two girls smiled and glanced at each other. Peter was not the only one to whom Spring had brought an appetite.

"May we sample a few and bring some in to the Alm-Uncle?" asked Jamy.

"So that's it!" laughed Brigitte, handing her a full plate. "Well, off with you or there will be none left for Peter."

"The greedy boy! You spoil him disgracefully," Heidi scolded. "When we have a child in the house you will not be saving so many for Peter."

Brigitte looked up, an anxious expression coming into her face.

She placed her hands on her ample hips and stood for a moment looking steadily at Heidi.

"Well," she said with a sigh, "the pillow and the little shirts are ready. I've been praying to the dear Lord that the child might arrive in good health before the strawberries blossom."

"Your prayers have been answered sooner than you expected," laughed Jamy. "It's my sister, Marta, that's coming, with your kind permission. But I'm afraid she's too large for the little shirts and pillow. She's nearly ten years old."

At this Brigitte sat back heavily on the stove bench and threw up both hands.

"And I thought you were talking about my own grandchild! The Lord has curious ways of granting our wishes. But all is for the best in His own good time. She will be a help with the baby when it does come. Is she the shy little one who marched ahead of the bride and groom at the wedding?"

"Yes. She's the one. The child that carried the wheat. And if your prayers bring results you might keep on praying that she arrives in good health. She's never been strong and all her life she has been a care to someone. Mama and Papa don't want her and she's written to ask if she may come and stay with me."

At first the kind-hearted Brigitte could not comprehend this.

"They don't want her, you say. What can be wrong with them that they don't want their own child?"

"Oh, I imagine Papa wants her," Jamy replied, "but he's too busy to take much notice. Our grandmother took care of her as long as she lived and Mama says she spoiled her. Anyway, they don't get along very well. I'm afraid I don't get along with them either," Jamy added. "Mama doesn't like to be seen with me for fear people will think she's old."

"Old? Well, isn't she?"

"Mercy, no!" Jamy replied. "She was only seventeen when I was born. She didn't look after me properly and so Grandma came to live with us. She took charge and even after Marta came, Mama and Papa still went to parties just as if they didn't have any children at all."

"I begin to see it now," said Brigitte, shaking her head at such a state of affairs. "Well, let the little sister come and welcome. She'll be needing someone to take that grandmother's place."

"You will do that, I know," cried Jamy, overjoyed, "and the Alm-Uncle will love her too. Come, Heidi, let's tell him about it right away."

"But first he must know that Spring is coming and that he will soon be well," said Heidi, following with the plate of cakes.

Chapter 2

The Expected Guest

*F*rom the kitchen a door at the left led into the Alm-Uncle's domain, while at the right another door exactly like it led into Heidi's bedroom. Thus the three rooms which had once been set apart as "winter quarters" for Heidi and her grandfather cuddled around the great kitchen stove as three chickens might seek warmth near mother hen. The stove itself formed part of the wall, making an attractive chimney corner in each of the bedrooms. Around these were benches on which three or four people might sit and warm their backs in the chill of winter.

The windows on this side of the house looked out on the mountain peaks while those in the living-room opened towards the valley. Here, also, was a stove which reached to the ceiling and warmed upstairs as well as downstairs. It was not open like the kitchen stove, but was tiled from top to bottom and on each separate tile was a picture in blue and white. This wonderfully decorated stove and the rich panelling which covered the walls made the living-room very pleasant in Winter. But the Alm-Uncle was used to simple surroundings and it was in an

ancient carved chair beside one of the windows in his own
room that he liked best to sit.

As Heidi and Jamy entered they could see him sitting there,
his face turned towards the rugged cliffs over which a cloud
hovered, shutting out his view of the glorious Alpine sunset. At
first the room was curiously darkened, but as they approached
the window, the cloud broke and such splendour blazed forth
that for a moment they stood in their places and could not
move a step for fear of breaking the spell that was upon them.

Now the twin peaks of the Falknis took on a deeper hue,
changing to purple, but the Scesaplana beyond it was still a rosy
red. The glaciers shone in brilliant whiteness and every line was
traced as though some giant pencil had been drawn across the
sky. Heidi could not speak to the grandfather. It would have
been like interrupting a person at prayer. But softly she tiptoed
to his side and took the wrinkled hand.

"It's come," said she gently after the sky had darkened.

The old man turned, as if realizing for the first time that he
was not alone.

"What's come? Heidi, what are you saying?"

"The Spring, Grandfather. We've been waiting so long. But
now it has really come and soon we shall close up this big house
and go up to the Alm hut."   ◆

Heidi still called the grandfather's chalet "the Alm hut" for
that had been the name of the cowherd's hut where he had
lived when she first came to him. Now a fine new chalet had
taken the place of the old hut, but the name still clung to it just
as the name "Alm-Uncle" clung to the old man, even though
he was no longer the fearful hermit of the mountains.

"Wait a little," he said. "Don't be in such a hurry. Spring

takes his time and the Alm is still covered with snow. There is not a patch of green to be seen above Dorfli."

"But below, in Maienfeld, the flowers are already blooming."

"The mountains are like an old man," said the Alm-Uncle, shaking his head. "It takes a long time to warm them. Don't plan too much for your old grandfather, Heidi. The Alm hut can get along very well this year without him."

"But, Grandfather!" cried Heidi, getting down on her knees beside him in the old way. "You always wanted to go up before. You never wanted to wait for the first patch of green to show on the slope. Remember how impatient you were to be up there when I was away at school and none of us wanted you to go alone? Now you will never have to go up there alone, Grandfather. There will be a family of us to go with you. Surely, by strawberry time, we will be able to take the children. There will be two of them—a child of our own and Jamy's little sister. She is coming to live with us and go to school. But in June school will be out and perhaps we can take them both to the high pastures——"

Heidi stopped then, for the grandfather was no longer listening. He had closed his eyes and sat dozing in his chair while she talked. That was not like him. She glanced anxiously at Jamy.

"Let's go now," Jamy said. "He's tired now and it may not be a good time to tell him about Marta. He may not agree with you, Heidi, for after all my sister is a stranger. Perhaps we had better see what Peter thinks about it first."

"You're right," said Heidi, "I would not do anything against Peter's wishes. But wouldn't it seem odd to you for a family to welcome a child of their own—a happy, healthy child who had never seen trouble, and turn away a strange child who really needed a home?"

"Everyone doesn't see these things in the generous way that you see them," replied Jamy, beginning to be apprehensive for it seemed to her that her little sister had brought nothing but trouble to those who had tried to take care of her.

"But Peter will. I'm sure he will," said Heidi with confidence.

Nothing more was said to the Alm-Uncle about the expected visitor and he was left to doze, while Heidi fixed a special treat to tempt his appetite. She brought it to him on a tray but he waved her away with his hand, saying briefly:

"Your old grandfather is tired, Heidi. Today food does not tempt him nearly as much as sleep."

Peter came in later and he, also, was tired. He and old Gaffer, the horse that had belonged to the doctor, had been in the valley all day ploughing a field. The frost was all out of the ground, he said, and the field was now ready for planting.

On the way home Peter had picked a few blossoms for Heidi and she wore one in her hair while she served his late supper. Black bread, sausage, cheese, and the round cakes his mother had made were set out on the table before him. Heidi then poured two glasses of goats' milk and touched them together, saying:

"To the health of our new guest, Marta."

Peter looked at her long and steadily. He had completely forgotten the name and had no idea who the guest was to be until Heidi explained that it was Jamy's little sister.

"But she is a sickly child!" he exclaimed. "You must not consider such a thing at a time like this when you should be saving all your strength for the care of your own baby. Do you realize that you will have no help from such a child? Do you not see that you will only be adding another burden to your

own shoulders? I remember well how pale and unhealthy Jamy's
sister appeared when she brought her here for the wedding."

"I remember it too," said Heidi. "I do not expect help from
the child. I expect to help her."

"Then you have already planned for it? You have already
decided?"

Heidi nodded, watching him as he helped himself to a thick
slice of sausage.

"A large house is meant to share, I suppose," he said grudg-
ingly. "But will I never have you to myself? First it was Clara;
then the doctor and then Chel, the waif we followed to his
hide-out in the mountain cave——"

"And look what happiness that brought us!" exclaimed Heidi.
"It was on that day we discovered our enchanted garden and
only think what a fine boy Chel has turned out to be. You
cannot regret that, Peter."

"But surely, Heidi, you have done enough for others and
soon we will have our own family to consider——"

"You haven't changed a bit, have you?" asked Heidi. "Do
you remember how you shook your fists behind the poor doctor's back when he first came to visit, and yet it is because of
him that we have this fine house and the horse and stable. Who
knows but what the child that is coming may bring the same
good fortune? What is it the song says?

> 'Gladness we send into the hearts of others
> Throws happy echoes back into our own' "

"Bring your violin and play it," Peter said. "It sounds better
with music and I can enjoy the little cakes even more."

Heidi fingered the instrument lovingly for a moment. Then

she played the song, softly at first, while Peter listened. The words must have been running through his mind for when the music was finished he drew her to him and said:

"If that is true, Heidi, some day you will be a princess in a palace. You do so much for others and never once think of yourself."

"Oh, but I shouldn't want to be a princess!" cried Heidi, as though alarmed at the thought. "It hurts me even now that I should have a nicer house than the other villagers. There simply isn't any way to make up for it unless we share it. You see, Peter, if we invite strangers into our house it won't be so empty. Even your mother is looking forward to the time when we will have a child to brighten up our home. This way we won't have to wait. Jamy's sister can be like our own daughter. She's so lonely, and I'm sure I shall love her."

"I'm sure you shall," said Peter a bit grimly. "When shall I have old Gaffer and the wagon ready to fetch her?"

"Peter, you are a dear!" cried Heidi, and flung her arms around his neck and hugged him until he could hardly get his breath.

Just then Jamy came into the kitchen.

"Oh, excuse me," she said, and started to go out again, but Heidi stopped her.

"Have you written to your sister?" she asked excitedly. "Tell her to take the train to Maienfeld as soon as possible and let us know what train she is taking because Peter is going to meet her with the wagon. He says he will. Isn't it marvellous? I'll play our song of rejoicing again and you and Peter must sing it with me."

"Is it the song you were playing before? I don't know it," Jamy protested.

"Then Peter will sing it until you do know it. It starts like a hymn, but just listen! The melody grows merrier and merrier until you simply have to forget everything else and dance."

Saying this, Heidi drew the bow across the violin strings and began to play:

"Sing, brother, sing! For are not all men brothers?
Nor ever must we sing our song alone;
Gladness we send into the hearts of others
Throws happy echoes back into our own.
Sing la-de-o! la-de-o! La-de-oooo!"

"Are those the happy echoes?" asked Jamy, laughing and whirling with the melody as Peter continued the joyous yodelling.

Heidi played on, and soon both Peter and Jamy were whirling and dancing, back and forth, touching elbows, dipping, curtsying to each other and swinging to the right and to the left, until the whole manor house rang with merriment. They were unaware of the grandfather, his old eyes shining, there in the doorway, watching. He had left his chair for the first time that day.

"Good!" he applauded when they turned and noticed him. "That's what I've been needing. It pleases me to see you all so happy. Keep it up"

"Sit down and have some cakes while we dance," said Heidi, offering the plate on which, by some miracle, three cakes still remained. "We have reason to be happy, Grandfather. We're expecting a guest, a little girl who needs a home such as we have. That's why we're all singing and making merry. We want her to feel welcome. Her name is Marta. Did you hear me,

Grandfather?" For Heidi had discovered that she was speaking to his turned back.

The old man appeared to be lost in thought as he made his way back to his own room.

"I don't think he heard," said Peter, "but if he pays as little attention to Marta as he has to the rest of us lately it won't matter anyway. I'm afraid he's getting very feeble."

"How old is he?" asked Jamy.

"Well past eighty. He never told us exactly, did he, Heidi?" Peter asked.

"There's a great deal he never told us," she agreed. "I keep meaning to ask him, but whenever I mention the past it seems to make him so sad. I've always thought he had some great sorrow about which none of us knew. There were years and years, after his parents died, when nobody knew where he was or anything about him. Some say his wife was a girl from a distant country and others insist she was from the Grisons. Nobody really knows. She must have met some sort of tragic death, for the first anybody knew of Grandfather he appeared in the Domleschg valley with my father, Tobias, and tried to find a home among his relatives there. Dete says they all turned him away because he had been such a reckless youth. The story is that he squandered his parents' whole fortune although I never did believe that. It was after he had been turned away from Domleschg that he came to Dorfli. Some of the villagers here are distantly related to him also. That's how it happens that they call him 'Uncle.' The family records go back for generations and all the nieces and nephews and cousins were displeased when Grandfather married a stranger and refused to tell them anything about her."

"He must have married after he left home to join the army in Naples," Peter put in. "He often tells us army stories and old legends."

"I know," Heidi replied thoughtfully. "It's only when we ask for stories of his own life that he grows so abrupt and silent."

"It's all very strange," agreed Jamy, "and it's a great pity not to know anything about your own grandmother. I knew mine very well and whenever other people didn't understand me I always ran to her. She was the kindest old lady. But I've told you about her before. She was the one who gave me the cross I always wear."

"Well, anyway, I had Peter's grandmother while she lived, and Clara's grandmamma in Frankfurt. I didn't mind borrowing my grandmothers," said Heidi more cheerfully. "Now all I ask is that you let me borrow your sister. You know, I never had a sister either."

"You're welcome to her," said Jamy with a little shrug. "Marta is often more of a trial than a blessing."

"But if she is really a trial," said Heidi thoughtfully, "might it not be only because she is unhappy?"

"She is very unhappy," Jamy agreed, "but the sad part of it is, she makes everyone else so. Sometimes Mama goes into a fit of crying when she can't cope with Marta's tantrums, and you, Heidi, must consider yourself and the little one that is coming——"

"I am doing that, Jamy," said Heidi softly, "but in my own way."

Chapter 3

The Arrival of Marta

*O*n the day that Marta was to arrive Heidi was up before sunrise preparing Peter's breakfast. She and Jamy were to accompany him to the railway station in Maienfeld and, to the delight of all the school children in Dorfli, Jamy had given them a half day's holiday so that she might meet her sister.

There was plenty of room for Marta in the blue wagon to which old Gaffer had been hitched. For, besides the high front seat, there was a soft hay bed in the back and one could ride there almost as comfortably as beside the driver. Milk cans, cheese, eggs and poultry usually rode to market in the back of the wagon.

"Are we ready?" asked Jamy, coming downstairs wearing a hat and cape. She stood in the doorway to the living-room and called out the question.

"Almost," Heidi replied, hurrying for her own wraps. "Peter is just finishing his breakfast in the kitchen. But have you had yours?"

"I had a cup of coffee. It's still too early to eat," declared Jamy, "and I am much too excited. I'm beginning to feel that perhaps Marta will be happy with us after all and that you may be able to do for her what nobody else can. You seem to be taking her troubles so to heart."

"I can't help it," said Heidi simply.

"I know it," cried Jamy in appreciation. "That is what makes it all so unbelievable. You really can't. You always take other people's troubles to heart. You suffer more for other people than you do for yourself. And I don't believe you've had breakfast either, just for thinking of Marta."

"You're right. I haven't," laughed Heidi. "But I wasn't hungry any more than you were. Later on all three of us can eat together. That will give me a chance to know your little sister better. I really must know what pleases her before I can make her feel at home."

Just then Peter called from the next room, where Heidi had placed a substantial breakfast of bread, cheese and sausage on the table. It was never too early for Peter to enjoy his food, but now he had finished and was anxious to be off. Gaffer was stamping and whinnying outside, as impatient as Peter. He was a handsome horse, with grey dappled spots on his back and a pure white forehead. His mane and tail were like fresh snow. But he was heavily built and looked curiously out of place hitched to the little blue wagon.

The sun was just rising in the East as they started. The two girls turned for a moment to admire the sunrise as they drove out of Dorfli. The valley below was still in darkness, but the high mountains, already bathed in light, made a magic circle around them. The early morning air carried a breath of snow and of pine forests.

"Look how fast the snow is melting on the Alps," cried Heidi, pointing to the patches of green on the slopes below the mountain peaks which were eternally capped with snow.

As they drove on, the broad white streaks could be seen only in the hollows and where the larch and fir trees had shaded the ground. Beyond, the trees were tall and black and appeared like sentinels around the village they were leaving. Farther up, on the distant slopes, the forests were shadowy masses of dark green.

The road was steep as it descended into Maienfeld. Now, at every turn, little flowers nodded. Pink and white crocuses, so delicate one could not pick them without their wilting, bloomed everywhere.

"Everything seems to be so alive just after sunrise," said Heidi. "Even the rocks appear to have faces."

"There's one saying 'good morning'," laughed Jamy, pleased at this fancy. "Look! You can see how the sun is gaining on us all the time. Now it's almost to Maienfeld. It will be there ahead of us."

A few chimneys were smoking as they drove past the first scattered houses and then into the main street of Maienfeld. Occasionally a cart rumbled by on its way to meet the incoming train. Now a whistle sounded. The train must be just crossing the covered railway bridge over the Rhine. Heidi hoped Marta would look out and see how queer it looked to have a long house built right over the river. She wondered if the child enjoyed new experiences as much as she did.

At first the train could be seen only as a puff of smoke in the distance. Nearer and nearer it came and soon the great wheels were turning almost in Heidi's ears. Marta looked very small and very much alone when Heidi first spied her on the platform. She was the only passenger to get off at Maienfeld. Heidi and Jamy both ran to meet her. Her sister held her close for a moment crushing the carefully brushed ringlets that hung about her shoulders. The child's little oval face seemed too small for the large eyes that looked about her so wonderingly.

"How was it?" asked Jamy, holding her away to look at her. "How did you leave Mama and Papa? How did you enjoy the trip?"

"All right," said Marta. "I left them all right."

"And you? Are you all right too?"

"Now that I'm here, I am. But I was so frightened on the train. If I hadn't wanted to come so badly I would never have let them put me on. You won't make me go back on the train, will you?" And the little girl looked pleadingly into her sister's face.

"No, dear," Jamy reassured her, "I won't make you go back. You are to live with Heidi, just as I do, and attend my school."

"Always?" asked Marta anxiously.

"As long as I teach," said Jamy.

The little face clouded and Heidi spoke quickly to reassure her:

"And I'm sure that will be a very long time."

Then Peter took one of her suitcases in either hand and her travelling bag under his arm and started towards the wagon.

"Come along!" he called. "Old Gaffer is waiting. Would you like to sit on the high seat with me while I drive him or back there in the hay?"

Marta considered this a moment as though it were a matter of great importance.

"I'd like to sit with you," she said shyly, "but I'd *love* to sit in the hay. Does it make any difference?"

"Not a particle," laughed Peter. "But be sure to hold on so you don't slide out when we start climbing the steep road to Dorfli."

Marta had hardly climbed into the back of the wagon when
she discovered that she had company. In a crate beside her
were several young chickens and she amused herself by poking
in her fingers and then drawing them quickly away for fear of
being bitten. The chickens cackled and jostled each other in
the crate but nobody said much of anything. The ride through
the ancient walled town of Maienfeld, past vineyards and gently
rolling fields and then up, up to where the snow still lay deep in
the purple shadows underneath the fir trees, was an experience
which called for silence. Glancing back, Heidi saw that Marta
was no longer paying any attention to the chickens. She had
lifted her face to the glorious mountains with their glistening
peaks and awe-inspiring glaciers. Of what was she thinking?
Did they thrill this little stranger as they had always thrilled
her? Would she, too, learn to love them?

"Don't they ever fall down?" Marta asked abruptly and Heidi
realized that it might take her a long while to understand this
child.

"How could they?" Jamy asked after a moment.

"Well," said Peter, taking a more practical view of the question,
"I have heard of mountains falling. Remember the story the
Alm-Uncle tells of how Mont Taurus fell on the little hamlet of
Epaune and swallowed up every inhabitant? Then there was the
mountain of Noviorroz which fell into the Rhone valley with
such a crash that the sun was hidden for more than an hour.
Some people say the Lake of Geneva was formed by such a
crash and that is why, even now, the waters of the lake are
forever changing and forming pictures of castles and hamlets
which are no longer there. Sometimes you can see boats sailing
upside down through the sky——"

"Stop it, Peter!" cried Jamy. "Wherever you learned all this,

I'm sure I don't know. But can't you see you're frightening my sister?"

"She asked a question and I was simply answering it."

"Let him go on!" panted Marta. "It's awful, but I like to hear it. We used to live near the Lake and it did look just as if fairies were flying about in the mist. It wasn't like these mountains. They look all sugary, like cake frosting, and *that* slides off."

"I wouldn't worry about it if I were you, Marta," Heidi put in. "A little later on, when the snow on the path is melted, you may go right up to the edge of those glaciers and touch them if you like. Then you'll see how solid they are. You can pick strawberries almost at the edge of them."

"Really?"

This seemed more impossible to Marta than Peter's upside down boat, for she knew he had only been describing the mirages which are often seen on Lake Geneva.

"How long does it take the snow to melt?" Marta asked presently.

"Not long," Heidi answered. "The slopes ought to be quite clear by the middle of May, although the strawberries don't ripen until June or July."

This gave Marta something new to think about and she asked more and more questions about strawberry picking, about the flowers and about the goats that lived in the high pastures at the edge of the glaciers, until, finally, Peter stopped the wagon in front of the manor house.

"Is this where you live?" asked Marta in surprise. "I thought it was up there." And she pointed to the Alm hut perched on the slope high above them, alone under its three fir trees.

"I did live there when you were here for the wedding," Heidi explained. "But now Peter and I live in this beautiful house that once belonged to the doctor."

"Where's the doctor now?" asked Marta unexpectedly.

Jamy shook her head and Heidi replied:

"He's gone away to another country—a very far country—so now we live here because he wanted us to."

"Did you buy the house then?"

"No, dear. He left it to us."

"Why don't you say he's dead then? He is dead, isn't he? People don't leave their houses to other people unless they're dead."

Heidi winced. It sounded so cruel coming from the lips of a little child. Dead to her, meant what happens to birds one finds in the fields. It hadn't happened to the doctor whom she loved. He was alive somewhere, she knew. And yet she nodded and answered very softly, "Yes, he's dead."

Marta hesitated a moment before she entered the house. Heidi thought she saw her shiver a little although the bright sun had taken away the early morning chill. Jamy and Peter followed, the latter carrying Marta's bags.

The great oaken door at the front of the house opened directly into the large living-room with its high ceiling and dark panels and its wonderful blue and white tile heating stove. Beyond it was the pleasant kitchen from which came the delightful odours of a second breakfast Brigitte was preparing for the returning travellers.

Marta was drawn towards the kitchen by the spicy odour and it was not until after she had been welcomed by Brigitte and had finished her seed cakes that Heidi could persuade her to go in and greet the Alm-Uncle.

He looked up at her timid "How do you do?" spoken in French as this was the tongue she was accustomed to using.

"Don't you speak our language?" he demanded. And all the while his piercing black eyes seemed to Marta to be drilling a hole right through her.

"I speak only a little," she answered, still in French. "I used to speak German and Hungarian too when I lived with my grandmother, but that was a long time ago and now I have forgotten."

"Well, try it anyway. It will come back to you. Can't you shake hands with an old man and tell him your name?"

"My name is Marta," she replied in German. But she still held her hands behind her back. Her nails were digging into the palms and she was trembling to her very toes.

The Alm-Uncle gave a start and looked at her even more closely. Then he turned abruptly to Heidi.

"Nobody told me that a child named Marta was coming here. Where have you found her?"

"She's Jamy's sister," Heidi replied. "We've been expecting her for several days. I tried to tell you."

"You told me nothing," he said, sitting in his chair like a rock and still staring at the child.

"But you've seen her before," Heidi insisted. "She was here for the wedding. Don't you remember?"

"I remember the child, but not the name. Nobody ever told me her name."

"I'm sorry, Grandfather," said Heidi. "But can the name matter such a great deal? We didn't mean to keep anything from you."

'No, no," he said, shaking his head and leaning back in his

chair. "It doesn't matter. Nothing matters. Take her away now. I want to rest."

Marta was only too willing to go. She had stood before those searching eyes until she felt stripped of all her secrets. The old man could read her mind. Of this she felt convinced. All the times she had thought mean, hateful thoughts; the doubts she had; all the fears; all were known to him and it would be better if she kept out of his way. She did not speak until after Heidi had shown her to the guest room upstairs and they were busy unpacking her things. Then she burst forth with unexpected violence:

"I hate your grandfather. He has eyes just like an eagle."

"Marta!" cried Heidi, too taken aback to say anything further until she had composed herself and put away the folded clothes that had been in her hands. Then she continued more calmly:

"Hate is a strong word for a little girl to use. Has anybody ever told you what the Good Book says about hating?"

Marta shook her head and lowered her eyes.

"It says that if you hate anyone you walk in darkness and if you stumble no one will lift you up, because hating another person is exactly like hating the dear Lord for He is in us and we in Him——"

"Does it really say that?" asked Marta, opening her eyes very wide. "Does it really say that hating a person is just like being blind?"

"Worse," said Heidi. "I once knew a blind woman who had love in her heart and she was a great deal happier than many of us who can see."

"I'm not happy," said Marta. "I don't think the Lord is in me at all, for lots of times I hate people and they hate me. And I do hate your grandfather," she added stubbornly, "and I don't think the Lord is in him either or he wouldn't have looked at me like that."

"You simply don't understand him," said Heidi, taking the child's hand. "But we won't hate each other anyway, will we, Marta?" And she gave the hand an affectionate little squeeze.

Suddenly warmed through by this unexpected tenderness, Marta pressed her face against Heidi's sleeve and began to cry.

Her sobs sounded louder and louder and soon Jamy, busy correcting papers at the desk downstairs, heard them and came hurrying up.

"I knew it!" she exclaimed. "No sooner does she get inside the house than she begins to have a tantrum——"

"This isn't a tantrum," said Heidi gently. "She's tired and it may do her good to cry a little. Just leave her with me, Jamy, and go back to your papers."

"Very well," said the sister, "but I think you have your hands more than full. Let her wear this. This may comfort her. It belonged to her grandmother."

And, with that, Jamy removed the cross she always wore and slipped it around Marta's neck.

"Oh!" she exclaimed in the middle of a sob. "Oh, it's Grandma's cross!"

Suddenly she threw her arms about Jamy's neck and kissed her and thanked her with all her heart.

"I won't walk in darkness if I wear this, will I? And I can't hate anyone while I'm wearing Grandma's cross!"

"Then keep it," said Jamy, and walked away quickly before she could change her mind. The cross had been her dearest possession and, much as she loved her little sister, it was not easy for her to part with it.

Chapter 4

New Experiences

*T*he next day the sun lighted up a magnificent landscape. The Falknis glistened, almost unreal, under a deep blue sky while the streams flowed everywhere through the meadows around Dorfli where the snow was melting. Marta pulled on her heavy boots for today she was to go down the slushy road to the school where her sister taught.

Dorfli was built in a hollow between the steep slopes that seemed to fold, one over the other, as they rose higher and higher to the Alpine pastures and beyond, to the glaciers and snow-capped pinnacles. The road which was deeply rutted and difficult to follow descended steeply past the church with its slender spire, the parsonage beside it, the few shops and then the school. But to reach the school one had to climb up again from the road for it was built like most of the scattered houses, as though someone had dropped it and it had just happened to cling to the steep slope where it was now standing.

Jamy felt a little uneasy as she took her sister's hand and trudged along beside her. How would the peasant children receive this newcomer who knew so little of their ways? She had often heard them shouting taunts to one another. What would Marta think when she heard their mocking, "Ach, der Liebling!" Would they dare call her the teacher's pet just because they were sisters?

This thought caused Jamy to make a resolution then and there. No matter what happened, she would never treat Marta any differently than she treated the others. If she disobeyed she would receive the same punishment. If she failed to complete her lessons she would, like the others, be kept after school.

"It's going to be difficult teaching my own sister," she said as though speaking to herself.

"Is it?" asked Marta, who was taking in everything with eager, wide-awake eyes. "Must I always speak in German now? Do all the other children?"

"Most of them speak both French and German," Jamy replied. "Your speech will improve with practice. You will need some helping at home if you wish to make rapid progress."

"But I can read it hardly at all."

"You will be happier in the lower classes at first. The older boys are much too rough. And you are small for your age."

"I won't let anybody think I'm stupid. I can speak Hungarian too," declared Marta, stamping her boot in a puddle of mud and accidentally spattering Jamy's skirt.

Arriving in the classroom she was given a seat which she was to share with another girl who had not yet arrived. Jamy always came ahead of the children but, later on, if she liked, Marta might come with her schoolmates. Dame Barbel's daughter, Erna, might like to walk with her since she was the one who would share her seat.

As the school children came in one after another they cast curious glances in Marta's direction. She sat stiffly in her seat as much as to say, "I am the teacher's sister. You don't dare speak to me."

Of course, Marta was not thinking anything of the kind. In her heart she was very anxious to have these new schoolmates like her. She only sat like that because everything was new and frightening to her. Even Jamy, up there behind the high desk with the blackboard behind her, was far from being the gentle sister she was at home.

Marta had a slate on which she copied everything she was told, but the figures were not as easy to add as they had been in other schools. It was only because her hand trembled and because Jamy spoke to her just as sharply as she did to the others and rapped on her desk with the ruler to call her to attention.

Twice, during a recitation, she answered in French although she knew she should have answered in German. Then, in French class where she really knew far more than the others, she answered in German and Jamy had to mark the answer wrong.

Several children laughed at her mistakes. Others hid their heads behind their geographies and that was worse than laughing. They might be making faces, for all Marta knew. The thought of those strange children making faces at her behind their geographies caused her to stammer and stumble over her lessons worse than ever. She felt her face burning and knew it must be as red as a cherry. But in sewing class she redeemed herself a little. Nothing could ever make her forget the neat stitches her grandmother had taught her. The class was sewing little shirts for the children in the Maienfeld hospital and the thought that she was doing something for someone else pleased Marta. Too soon, the sewing class was over and she was being

asked questions concerning the history of Switzerland. Now she
stammered more than ever over her answers.

The children ran out without asking her to join them at
recreation and she imagined they were all whispering unkind
taunts behind her back. But somehow, she got through her first
day at school and came home with all her books determined to
learn her lessons so well that they would be forced to admire
her. If she didn't go out at recreation there would be all the
more time left for study.

"Well, how did it go?" asked Heidi, meeting her at the door.

Marta sighed deeply. "I could hardly bear it. Everything was
different and nobody spoke to me."

"How was that?" called the Alm-Uncle from his room. His
hearing was keen and again Marta was seized with the fear that
he could read her thoughts.

"And did you expect them to speak to you first?" he called
again. "Does anyone speak to a child who appears half frightened
out of her senses and sits at play-time with her face in her book?"

"How did he know that?" gasped Marta. "Who could have
told him that?"

"He knows a great many things without being told," Heidi
replied. "He understands how a little girl feels in a strange
school and can easily guess what she will do. But tomorrow you
must not sit with your face in a book. You must run out with
the others and, if they do not speak to you, then speak to
them. I'm sure they will answer."

This cheered Marta a little. Perhaps the other children hadn't
laughed behind their books any more than she had. Perhaps
they, too, were frightened and were waiting for her to speak.
The following day, when recreation came, Marta did as Heidi
had suggested and when she came home that evening she had

quite a different story to tell. She had spoken to her seat-mate several times during the afternoon. In fact, they had whispered so much that it had been necessary for Jamy to correct them.

"And then," Marta continued, "it seemed as if everybody changed. I don't mind being corrected any more because Erna said she thought I'd be the teacher's pet, but now she knows I'm not and so she likes me."

The Alm-Uncle had been listening to this animated account of the day at school but he said nothing. A little later, however, when Marta was studying her history lesson he heard her stumbling.

"Come here, child, and let me show you how it goes," he offered.

Marta looked about as though searching for a means of escape. But, as there was none, she grasped her cross tightly in both fists and came.

"You've forgotten your book, dear," Heidi reminded her.

"She won't need a book," the Alm-Uncle replied quickly. "She has had enough of books. All day they have crowded around her like a vast army and she has had enough of doing battle with books."

Marta glanced up wonderingly. How could he know that each book had seemed to possess its own little spear with which to stab her? but then she remembered Heidi's words: "He understands how a little girl feels." This reassured her. Once her grandmother had said she understood. Perhaps they both did. Old people, thought Marta, must be very wise having lived so many years and it occurred to her that it was not at all wise to be afraid of anyone as feeble as the poor uncle. His eyes were sharp, to be sure, but he went on speaking in a kindly manner:

"Books are all right in their place, but now school is over and it is time the child learned her lessons in another way."

"Is there another?" Marta managed to ask.

"To be sure," he answered. "How do you suppose children learned their lessons before there were any books?"

Was there ever such a time? Marta wondered. But now she was quite curious. Overcoming her fear, she let the cross fall back in its place and came closer.

"How did they?" she asked, almost in a whisper.

"I think pictures came before books," said the Alm-Uncle, "and stories before pictures. But your history does not go back as far as that. It begins, like this, with three cantons. Switzerland is divided into cantons, you see, just the way this apple is divided. These are the first three." And he placed three pieces of dried apple on the stove bench. "This is Uri. This is Schwyz and this is Unterwalden," he continued, naming each piece separately. "Now these three united and swore allegiance——"

"What's that?" interrupted Marta, now completely fascinated by his explanation.

"It's a promise," he said. "The men of these three cantons promised to help each other just as a husband and wife do when they take each other's hand in marriage. But they were Swiss and a Swiss soldier never breaks his promise."

Marta looked up, surprised at the changed tone of his voice. Once more his eyes reminded her of an eagle's. He was no longer explaining her history lesson but simply staring into space as though seeing something that had happened long ago. Marta waited a moment, hoping he would go on explaining her history lesson, but as he continued to sit there lost in thought, she took the pieces of apple and went out.

"Uri, Schwyz, Unterwalden," she repeated over and over to herself and not until she had thoroughly learned them did she so much as taste the delicious dried apple.

Chapter 5

Marta Recites a Prayer

*T*he April weather was changeable, one day always being exactly the opposite of the day which followed it. If the sun shone very brightly one day, the following day would bring thick, dark clouds and the rain would pour down the slope into dozens of little rivulets.

Quite often, on rainy days, Marta would be seen at the Alm-Uncle's side with her slate, pencils and school books. She was afraid not to come when he called her. But gradually, her fear of him changed into admiration and respect. If anything troubled her he saw to it that everything was set to right and if her lessons puzzled her, his explanations made it all clear. Often, when there were errands to be run, he would send for her. It tired him to climb the stairs and he no longer attempted it.

"The child can get it," he would say and, as time passed, she ran his errands more and more willingly. Heidi, too, sometimes sent her to the store and Brigitte let her pat out the little cakes she baked in the kitchen. At school she was allowed to wash blackboards, clean erasers and put away the chalk. Thus, for the first time in her life, she began to feel that she was of some use and was no longer a burden.

"You bring back my strength," the Alm-Uncle said to her one day when she ran to him with her lessons. "Sometimes I think the dear Lord lets us stay on earth as long as we are needed. He sees that you and I are helping each other."

"Does He?" asked Marta, looking up into the old man's face.

"Indeed He does," he replied, nodding wisely. "Sometimes again I think He sent you to me. He has a marvellous way of working out everything for the good of His children here on earth."

"Tell me more," pleaded Marta. "How do you know about Him when He is so far away?"

"He is near, if we have Him in our hearts, child. But I know how it is. There was a time when He was far away from me also. I had gone to a distant country to become a soldier and when I returned home both my parents were dead. My wife was gone and there was only the boy left to me. He married and after a few years he and his wife were taken too. I called upon God to help me but then it seemed that He was very, very far away."

"Then how did you find Him?" asked Marta, placing her head against the old man's knee.

"Through Heidi," he said. "She told me a story. But the Master Himself has told us how to find Him. Once, long ago, a man followed Him and called out, 'Good Master, what shall I do that I may enter Heaven?' And the Master said, 'Why callest me good? There is none good but One and that is God. Obey Him and keep His commandments.' Then the man answered, 'All His commandments I have kept from my youth.'

"But hear this, child. The man in our story was a very rich man. The Master knew this and said to him, 'Sell everything you have and give to the poor; then you shall have treasures in Heaven.'

"Hearing this, the man went away sadly, for he had great possessions and would not give them up. Then the Master said to those that had gathered about Him, 'Children, how hard it is for them that trust in riches to enter the Kingdom of God!' "

"Grandma told me that story once," said Marta. "But she said something about a camel and a needle's eye and I didn't understand it."

"That follows. He said that too."

"Do you know any other stories?" asked Marta. "Tell me more. I love to hear them."

And so it was that Marta was often seen sitting on her little stool at the Alm-Uncle's feet listening to his stories. Sometimes they were parables from the Bible but more often she heard legends which would help her to understand the history of Switzerland. One day she discovered, to her delight, that many of these stories were pictured on the wonderful blue and white tiled stove in the living-room.

"Come and see them, Uncle," she begged, taking his hand. "There are so many and I don't half understand them. There's one of a battle and one of horses and another where three men are holding up their hands——"

"Ah, but I know them without looking," he said. "Those are our friends, the three Swiss who kept their promise."

And he went on to explain the other pictures, telling her how the stove had been placed in the manor house years before by the wealthy soldier who had built it.

"In those days," he said, "many adventurous young men of Switzerland were ready to help to fight other nations' battles for them; for wealth or for glory or for the love of some woman.

Today they are much wiser. They fight only to defend our borders and preserve the peace."

"Didn't you say you were once a soldier?" Marta asked eagerly.

"I was," he replied, "and as foolish as the rest of them."

"Did you fight for wealth or for glory or——"

"Bah!" he interrupted so violently that she gave a little start and clutched her cross, as it had come to stand between her and the things she feared. "We are talking about this soldier," he continued. "This brave young man who came home from foreign lands to lay up his treasures in Dorfli. You see how little he cared for his home. It would have fallen apart from neglect if nobody had troubled to repair it."

"But people did trouble, didn't they?" asked Marta, trying to follow the story.

"My son and I were the first to work on it. Then Andre, the village carpenter, repaired it further for the doctor. It's pretty solid now," he added, grasping a beam and shaking it until the child trembled for fear the whole structure would fall on her head.

"What's the matter? Have you no faith?" he demanded.

"Faith in what?"

"In me. In Heidi. In the Lord Himself and the people He has created. There's nothing to make a little girl tremble like that if only she has faith."

"Then I suppose I don't have," Marta admitted. "Ever since Grandma died I've been afraid of everything. But she was brave and it helps a little to wear her cross."

"Come here, child, and let me see it. I never looked at it closely before."

Marta came and stood quietly as he examined the cross Jamy had given her. He looked at it once; then held it nearer and looked again. After that he turned it over so that the under side could be plainly seen. Here the thin gold edges gave the cross the appearance of a cross-shaped pastry cutter or baking dish and it was clear that another half had once fitted into the half over her locket. It wasn't pretty on the other side. The Alm-Uncle looked at it a long time before he spoke.

"The hinge is broken," he said gruffly.

"I didn't break it," Marta hastened to tell him. "It was broken when Grandma had it."

"And did she ever tell you who broke it?"

"Not exactly," Marta confessed, "but she liked it this way. My grandfather gave it to her years and years ago and she said whenever she looked at it she thought of the Master's words: 'Come, take up my cross and follow me.' That was when she told me about the needle's eye and how a rich man could as easily go through it as through the Gates of Heaven. That was her favourite Bible story. It's funny how you knew it too."

"Everybody knows it," said the Alm-Uncle.

"I like your way of telling it almost as well as Grandma's," said Marta, as she thoughtfully fingered her cross.

"She must have had a hard life, this grandmother of yours," the Alm-Uncle remarked after a moment.

"I suppose she did," Marta agreed. "But she never told me that. She was so kind and good. I thought at first I would die without her, for she taught me every good thing I know."

"Well then," demanded the uncle, "and did she not teach you faith?"

"I suppose she did," Marta admitted. "She taught me to say my prayers."

"And do you say them?"

"Not the long one. I only say, 'God keep me' very quickly and jump into bed."

The Alm-Uncle scowled very fiercely at this and his bushy eyebrows came closer together.

"And do you suppose the grandma would have troubled to teach you the long prayer if she did not wish you to say it?"

Marta was trembling again.

"You—you don't say it. You sing it."

"All the better," said the Alm-Uncle. "You must sing it every night."

This was a clear command and Marta knew very well that she must do as she was told. That evening, after she had dressed herself in her ruffled nightgown and was ready to jump into bed, she paused for a moment and opened her mouth to sing. But the upstairs room was so quiet she dared not make a sound for fear the echoes would leap back at her like so many voices calling from the walls and the ceiling and even down the chimneys. Gathering the long nightgown about her, she scurried downstairs and found Heidi in the Alm-Uncle's room.

"He told me to sing the prayer that Grandma taught me," she said, pointing to the old man who appeared to be dozing in his chair. "But I can't sing it. I tried and the words won't come."

"Perhaps I could help you," Heidi offered. "If I knew the tune I could play it on my violin."

"I'll show you how it goes."

And now that Heidi was there and the lamp she had brought in lighted every corner of the room, both the words and tune came easily:

> *"I need a kinder heart;*
> *Dear Spirit, dwell in me,*
> *Help me to live and love and work*
> *And of more service be."*

The Alm-Uncle had turned his head and was listening now. Jamy and Brigitte had come in and quietly seated themselves on the stove bench. Heidi took up her violin for she had now learned the tune, and the child went on in a clear, sweet voice:

> *"I need a stronger will;*
> *Eternal One Divine,*
> *Oh, strengthen me and make my thoughts*
> *In harmony with Thine.*
>
> *"I need a broader mind;*
> *Dear Spirit, make me see*
> *That all who struggle here in pain*
> *Are labouring for Thee."*

Brigitte looked at her work-worn hands and smiled as if the hymn had given her work a new meaning.

"And now comes the part about faith," Marta announced with a deep sigh, for it seemed to her that the prayer was very, very long.

"Well," said the Alm-Uncle, "let's have it."

What was there about the hymn that made him look so fierce, Marta wondered. But she continued to sing, thankful that this was the last verse:

> *"I need a purer life;*
> *Dear Spirit from above.*
> *Drop Thy still dews of faith and peace*
> *And Thy eternal love."*

A long silence followed. Marta stood there in the centre of the room, as still as a mouse herself, but she was glancing anxiously from one face to another wishing that she could read their thoughts as well as she had learned to read the language they spoke.

Heidi was the first to say anything.

"Marta," she breathed, "your prayer was beautiful. I'm sure the dear Lord heard it and thought so too."

"But I wasn't singing it for Him," said Marta, bewildered. "I was singing it for you."

"In that case," said the Alm-Uncle gruffly, "you may as well continue to pray 'God keep me' until you learn what this means."

"Oh, thank you!" cried Marta. To her, "God keep me" was a much more sensible prayer as all sorts of things might happen to a person in the night.

Chapter 6

A Double Blessing

*B*y the end of April the warm south wind had blown the last bit of snow from the sunny slopes, bringing with it a bright trail of flowers. Heidi had promised Marta that there would be a surprise for her when the strawberries bloomed and often she sat quietly on the bench in the garden wondering what it would be.

Perhaps Thoni, the goat boy, would take her to the high pastures with him. But Marta wasn't at all sure of this as the boy paid little attention to her in school. He was in the highest class and regarded the small girls as too unimportant to be noticed. Still Marta waited eagerly for the time when the goats would go up to the high pastures wearing flowers on their horns and tinkling bells about their necks.

Every day Peter could be seen on the steep hillside ploughing his fields for the Spring planting. Later on, if his crops yielded as well as he expected, he planned to buy a fine herd of brown cows and pasture them on the Alm. He and the Alm-Uncle had talked it over and both agreed that there was no profit in making goat cheese. It spoiled too quickly to be shipped any great distance and he had difficulty selling it in Maienfeld or

Ragatz where many of the tourists had not acquired a taste for it. So, in order to buy his cows, he had sold all but four of his goats. He thought with satisfaction how the family would soon be using all the milk from these four and was thankful that he had kept them. He still had Meckerli, the white goat he had raised from a kid; Gitzi who gave such rich, creamy milk; Blitschnell (quick as lightning); and Tolpet (the foolish one), pure black and still crying for her mother. This last goat was Marta's pet. She knew exactly how it felt, for hadn't she lost the dear grandma who used to look after her? Often she had wanted to bleat as pitifully as did this little goat.`

"Poor little Tolpet," she cried compassionately, kissing it on its funny black nose. "I'll take care of you. I'll be your mother."

The kid stretched its neck and nuzzled so contentedly into her pinafore that she hugged it and kissed it again, repeating:

"I'll take care of you."

"Take it for a little run up the slope then," Peter told her. "It must learn to use its legs or it will not be able to keep up with the others when Thoni takes them to pasture."

"Is he going to take them soon?"

"Yes, certainly," said Peter. "As soon as school is out he will take all the goats in the village. He will call them together by blowing on a little horn—like this." And Peter took from a peg in the goat-shed a horn that he himself used when he was a goat boy.

"Would you like to try it?" he asked.

Marta set the horn to her lips and was surprised and delighted when the goats trooped after her.

"Look! Look!" she cried, leading them about where they could be seen from the Alm-Uncle's window. "They follow me! They really follow me!"

"So they do!" chuckled the Alm-Uncle, leaning far out to watch the happy child dancing about, just as Heidi had danced, with the goats around her.

"Listen!"

And now she blew a shrill note on the horn so that the goats all crowded together, their bells tinkling with such a queer, tinny tune that Marta laughed and shouted again:

"Look at the choir! Look at the funny goat choir!"

"That's more like it," said the Alm-Uncle, turning from the window. "Heidi!" he called. "Come here and watch the child."

"Oh, Grandfather!" cried Heidi, throwing a shawl over her shoulders in her haste to be out in the sunny fields with them. "I must go, too. I really must."

But in the yard Peter stopped her and placed his arm gently about her. "See, the child is running and enjoying herself with the goats just as we used to do. But if we have a son he will no longer tend the neighbours' goats, but his father's own herd of sleek brown cows. Many of the villagers are anxious to sell their land and move down to Maienfeld where there is work in the vineyards. So, you see, with what we already have and with a fine, strong boy to help us, we may yet own one of the largest farms this side of the Prattigau."

"That would please you very much, wouldn't it, Peter? And I'm glad you are planning," Heidi added, "but I did not know you wanted a son and so I have been praying that your baby will be a little daughter. A daughter is closer to the mother than a son and when Marta leaves I am afraid I shall be very lonely."

"I'm not leaving! I'm not leaving!" cried Marta passionately, for she had overheard the last of what Heidi was saying and had come tearing down the slope, almost falling over the startled

Tolpet. "Jamy and I are staying here all summer. She said so. She said you would need us and besides," she added, facing Heidi as though to hold her to her promise, "you said there would be a surprise for me when the strawberries blossomed and there's a whole field of blooms right here on the slope where Tolpet was grazing."

"Then pick one for me!" cried Heidi. "I will wear it in my hair this evening to show Peter that we have not long to wait."

Heidi wore the strawberry blossom, but long before evening, Peter was called home from the fields. He was even more surprised than Marta for, when he reached home, he found that he was already the proud father, not only of the boy he wanted but also of a girl.

In the living-room a great discussion was going on. The village dressmaker and the baker's wife as well as Dame Barbel and several other ladies were there. It seemed Heidi needed help in naming her babies for each one had a different suggestion.

"Twins should have names that sound alike," volunteered the village seamstress. "In Seewis, just over the mountains, there is a beautiful pair of twins and they are named Renz and Renzia. Barbel and Barbarossa would be two fine names. I believe you are distantly related——"

"Very distantly," interrupted a neighbour, who did not wish to see Dame Barbel thus honoured. "If they were my twins I should name them after a close relative."

"The boy will be called Peter, of course, after his father and grandfather," Dame Barbel offered as her opinion. "But they can't call the girl Heidi. It isn't a name. They can, perhaps, call her Adelheid."

"Adelheid! Her mother was a sleepwalker," protested one of

the older residents. "Surely it would not be right to call down such an affliction on the head of an innocent baby."

"Why not Dete after her mother's sister?"

With this the others were quick to disagree. Even Dame Barbel, who had been a friend of Dete's, thought this name quite out of the question. The aunt had deserted Heidi when she was only five years old. She had left her with the Alm-Uncle and their voices made this sound as though he were still a fearful old hermit. The seamstress added that but for Heidi he might still be living like an eagle up there on the rocks.

"But *Ursel!*" announced the baker's wife with a triumphant gleam in her eyes. "Now there's a name she might easily choose. Heidi was put out to board with a woman named Ursel. I've heard her mention it."

All at once a curtain in the room began to move. The ladies turned, horrified, to see a child suddenly burst out of this hiding place and face them with flashing eyes.

"Why, it's Marta, the schoolmistress's sister! Do you suppose she could have heard——"

"I heard everything!" exploded the child. "And you sha'n't name Heidi's baby Dete or Ursel or Adelheid or any of those horrid names. And why should the little boy be called Peter? There are too many Peters already."

"You're right about that," said Peter, who had arrived just in time to hear the end of Marta's speech. He took the little girl's arm and led her out of the room. "You'll excuse us, ladies," he told the visitors, "if we go in and consult with the mother."

In her bedroom, which was nearer the living-room than any of the gossiping ladies had supposed, Peter found Heidi and had his first look at the two infants. Brigitte presented them for his inspection, each buttoned to its own ruffled pillow. The tiny heads were no bigger than apples and the eyes were closed so tightly one could hardly see they were there.

"Well, what do you think of them, Peterli?" his mother asked after he had studied their features for some time without making any comment.

"As alike as two strawberries," he answered, "and just as red. How long will it be before their eyes open?"

"They aren't kittens," laughed Heidi, looking up from her pillows. "Their eyes have already opened and they're as blue as the sky itself. They're sleeping now. Little babies have to sleep."

"Has the Alm-Uncle seen them?" asked Peter, his face still thoughtful.

"Oh, yes," answered Heidi. "He was so pleased, but he escaped to his own room again as soon as the neighbours came. Their chatter bothers him as it does me, but I can't ask them to leave."

"I'll ask them if you want me to," announced Marta, her eyes still fiery. "They're out there in the living-room saying horrid things about everybody in the family and suggesting the most dreadful names for the babies. You won't name them anything they suggest, will you?"

"I swear it!" said Peter, raising his hand as though taking an oath. "Whatever they suggest, the babies shall surely be named something different."

Old age had not affected the Alm-Uncle's hearing for, suddenly, he called out so loudly that those in Heidi's bedroom and even the neighbours in the living-room beyond could hear it:

"If they're her surprise, why not name the girl baby after the child?"

"After me?" said Marta, hardly believing her ears for the

Alm-Uncle had never once spoken her name all the time she had been there.

"As you say, Grandfather!" Heidi called back. "But what shall we name the boy?"

"Your father was an upright man, Heidi. It might be well to remember him."

Heidi had not thought of naming the boy anything but Peter. But since Peter objected to that, why not Tobias? She called again:

"Very well, Grandfather. He shall be our little Tobi. The neighbours shall hear at the church what names we have chosen."

Chapter 7

The Christening

*I*t was Sunday, the day of the christening. The sun shed its warmth over the village while water from the melting snow rippled and gurgled throughout the meadows which were robed in green. Crocuses covered the slope like a tapestry, even spreading themselves to the church lawn so that one could hardly walk without bruising them. In the midst of this garden of crocuses stood the church from whose steeple sounded the ancient bell—now soft, now clear and ringing, calling people to services.

"Come, Heidi! Come, Heidi!" the bell seemed to call just as it had done on that long-ago Sunday when the little girl had walked proudly beside the grandfather in his coat with the brass buttons. That was the day he had come to repent of his youthful follies and to make his peace with God and the villagers. Often, in the years between that day and this joyful Sunday, he had been seen sitting silent and reverent in the pew.

Today the bell sounded far beyond the village. The twin peaks of the rugged Falknis and the snow-capped Scesaplana seemed to catch the notes and throw them back, adding an echo that spoke again, "Come, Heidi, come!" It was almost as if the dear Lord Himself were calling her.

For a moment Heidi stood with head lifted, breathless, watching the swinging bell. Then the heavy oak door of the manor house opened and she turned, expectant, as Peter came and stood beside her.

"Happy?" he asked.

"How could I be anything but happy on such a morning?" cried Heidi.

"I'm rather proud of the little rascals myself," said Peter. "It's a pity the doctor couldn't have lived to see them."

"He will see the christening from where he is," said Heidi with confidence. "It's the grandfather who will miss it. He hasn't strength enough to travel even as far as the church. But at least he's had the pleasure of naming his great-grandchildren."

"The villagers will wonder why we haven't named the little girl after a relative," Peter went on thoughtfully, "but Tobias ought to suit them. Your father must have been a brave boy to win over everybody in the village when so much was being said against the Alm-Uncle. I heard it when I was hardly this high." And Peter levelled his hand to a place just above his knee. "To my mind it was the village gossips who needed to repent, not your grandfather."

"They are kind neighbours now," said Heidi, always charitable. "There isn't one of them who hasn't brought some delicate piece of needlework, and their gossip means nothing, Peter, really nothing."

"I'm afraid it means something to Marta," Peter said thoughtfully. "She's always hiding and listening. She was behind the curtains on that day they were discussing the babies' names. By the way, shouldn't I go in and fetch them?"

"They're nearly ready!" called Jamy from the door. "Brigitte was not satisfied with the way Heidi had fixed them. Now she must tie each little bow. It is not often that the villagers witness such a christening."

"Not in my memory," said Peter proudly. "Heidi and I have been doubly blessed, thanks to your little sister who carried the wheat."

"Was it because of me?" asked Marta, pushing forward from behind her sister. Her face looked out from under a starched bonnet, giving her a quaint, doll-like appearance that matched her serious manner.

"I suppose it might have been," Peter answered. "A bunch of wheat is supposed to stand for a fruitful marriage. There are a great many things of the kind that are supposed to mean something at a wedding, and Heidi and I did want children."

Marta pouted at that. For a moment it seemed as though the babies had taken her place.

"I'm your child too," she reminded him.

"Then you must help care for the twins as a big sister should," laughed Heidi. "Run in now and see what's keeping their grandmother."

"Never mind. I will," said Peter, and in another moment the door opened again. This time it was Brigitte in her lace shawl and wide, silk apron. The grandmother of the children to be christened now turned and called in alarm:

"Not yet, Peterli! Not yet!"

"Such pet names are for the little ones now," sounded a voice from inside. "You must get used to it or you will have us confused and find yourself knitting little jackets for me. But what's the reason for not bringing them to their mother at once?"

"You must first take them up if you wish them to rise in the world," said Brigitte, still laughing.

"Very well," called Heidi, "take them up to the first landing and then bring them to me. It's nearly time for the service."

This was done and none of the others noticed that Marta was listening, her eyes very wide and serious.

At the church they were joined by other relatives, including Dete who appeared as haughty as ever. Her stylish clothes seemed out of place in the congregation of simple peasants. She was now working as chamber maid in a large hotel in Wallenstadt by the lake. Heidi heard all about it from the aunt's own lips after the service and with it a great deal of advice was offered in regard to the care of the twins. Dete, like many another maiden lady, seemed to know more about it than the mother herself, and Heidi was obliged to listen out of courtesy. But now there was nothing of this; only the deep-toned organ playing as Peter and Heidi entered the church. The proud father carried a baby on either arm and all eyes turned towards him. He had prophesied truly, for every villager in Dorfli was to be counted in the congregation, besides many strangers from Maienfeld and the outlying hamlets.

The organ played on, its tones swelling in Heidi's heart. Beside the pulpit was the christening font. Her eyes rested on it all through the service. Once she had wondered what a christening was, how it happened that her Christian name was Adelheid, when everybody called her Heidi. Her own babies might some day wonder about it as she had. She watched everything so that she might be able to tell them how they had come all dressed in lace to be consecrated to the dear Lord.

The church was perfumed with narcissi, as two bowls filled with these pure white flowers had been placed on either side of the pulpit. The pastor was the one who had persuaded the grandfather that it was right to send Heidi to school. He had welcomed them back to the village and she and Peter had often played at the parsonage with his children. He had been the one to hold the yoke over their heads and repeat the solemn words that had united them in marriage. This thought caused Heidi's eyes to fill with tears of happiness. What could be more fitting than that the same good man should christen her babies?

Across the aisle Jamy was sitting close to her little sister. Marta had never watched a christening and had seldom been inside a church. Her mamma and papa were always too busy to take her. Now she watched, round-eyed, as the pastor brought water and poured it in the font.

"What's that for?" she asked in a loud whisper.

"To christen the babies," Jamy whispered back, placing her fingers to her lips.

Unmindful of this, Marta whispered again, still louder than the first time, "But aren't the babies too big to fit in the bird bath?"

Jamy silenced her, but the whole congregation heard it and there was a ripple of suppressed laughter throughout the church.

The service was long and Tobi grew restless and whimpered a little, but finally the words came, and Peter and Heidi, each holding a baby, walked solemnly down the aisle and stood beside the font. Dipping his fingers into the water, the pastor now repeated each baby's name. First Tobi whose whole name, Tobias Peter Naegeli, sounded very impressive; then Marta Brigida Naegeli which would be shortened to Martali.

Little Tobi, as he felt the water upon his head, wrinkled his tiny nose and began to cry.

But Martali continued to sleep as though her name meant nothing.

"It is a good omen when a baby cries at a christening," one of the villagers pushed forward to tell Heidi, when they were outside the church and the beautiful service was over. But Heidi was still filled with a tender joy and hardly heard her.

"Why is it a good omen?" asked Marta, who was walking beside Heidi in order to be near her little namesake.

"Heidi, why is it a good omen?" asked Marta again when the villager failed to answer her question.

"It is only superstition," said Heidi. "Tobi cried because he was tired and when we reach home, you'll see, Tobi will be napping and then it will be Martali who is restless."

"But is it a *bad* omen because Martali didn't cry?"

"Perhaps the villagers will tell you that," said Heidi. "Dame Barbel and the others like to talk. But there is nothing in it. Tobi and Martali both have the dear Lord to guide them and need not fear either good or evil omens."

"I see," replied the child, but she still wore the same perplexed frown. The lonely Marta had already known trouble and had grown to expect it. Her father paid little attention to his children. Her mamma had made it quite clear that they were in the way. Jamy, naturally of a warm and trusting nature, had many friends to make up for this lack of a mother's affection. But Marta's starved little heart had found nothing to take its place. All sorts of fears began to crowd into her mind. Had something happened at her christening? Had somebody walked down with her instead of up? How many other unnamed things might happen to a baby she could hardly guess. Now she felt that Martali was her special charge and walked still closer to

her as more and more people crowded around to speak a word
with the mother of the twins.

Many of the villagers expressed surprise at the names which
had been chosen. Many others, especially those who had known
Heidi's father, were pleased that he had been remembered.
Among these was Andre, the village carpenter and son of the
man who had taught Heidi's father his trade.

"I shall surely visit the boy," he promised. "You have chosen
his name wisely. Perhaps he, too, will become a carpenter."

"Heaven forbid!" exclaimed Dete, who was standing near.
She had not forgotten that Tobias, the Alm-Uncle's only son,
had been killed while working on a house. She whispered
something of this to her friend, Barbel, little thinking that
Marta's sharp ears had taken in every word.

"I don't mind what trade he follows," Heidi said, "so long as
he has courage and does the best he can."

"Remember, I promise you a visit," the carpenter repeated.
"If the Alm-Uncle is ill he will welcome a friendly word or two
this afternoon. Surely he must be pleased with Tobi's name.
But where have you found the name for this little one who is
sleeping?"

"She's named for our Marta," replied Heidi, shifting the
sleeping Martali to the other arm and stroking the child's soft
curls. "She is the sister of the schoolmistress and both of them
board with us."

"Ah, so that is it. I had not heard the child's name before. I
thought . . . perhaps but the name is only faintly familiar. It
was not, as I supposed at first, a family name."

"The second name is for Peter's mother, Brigida or Brigitte as
she is called. Grandfather suggested Marta, although, for the
baby, it must be Martali. Is it not a beautiful name? Martali,"

Heidi repeated softly, her arm still about the wondering Marta.
"You see how musical it is. Some day our Martali may sing for
us as sweetly as Marta does."

"I'll teach her," volunteered Marta earnestly.

"I see you have a helper in the child," Dete said as she
moved away with Barbel whose husband was driving her back
to the station. "With babies to mind one does not run about
with the goats in the pasture."

"Oh, no. Certainly I will not run with the goats," Marta
responded quickly.

Chapter 8

The Carpenter's Gift

*Y*ellow coltsfoot blossoms edged the path from the church to the manor house and from all the shady places delicate pink and white anemones nodded gaily as though to greet the newly christened infants. Peter strode on ahead with Tobi but Heidi lingered, hoping Martali would wake and see the flowers.

"May I carry her now?" Marta asked over and over as she and Heidi trudged along. "There! Now there's only a few more steps and your Aunt Dete said I should help you look after the babies. Please may I carry Martali?"

Still Heidi hesitated. Martali, pillow and all, couldn't weigh more than eight pounds. But Marta looked so frail. Many young children in the village carried their little brothers and sisters about and thought nothing of it, but Marta was not intended for such work.

"Why don't you gather some flowers for her instead?" Heidi suggested. "Then, when we are home, you may place them in a glass beside her pillow so that she may look at them. I'm sure she's old enough to enjoy looking at flowers. Will you do that for her, Marta, and then run out to play?"

"I'll do it," said Marta, "but I'd rather stay beside her than play outside by myself. It's lonely outside——"

"Lonely!" exclaimed Heidi. "How could it be lonely with all these thousands of bright blossoms for company?"

"Flowers can't talk," Marta replied. "Even on Saturdays when I go to the pasture Thoni doesn't talk much. He just lies on the grass and lets the goats butt one another and bleat. Your Aunt Dete is right. I should not run with the goats. I should stay with the babies and—and be of service."

"Very well then," said Heidi, "when the babies are in the garden you may stay with them. But soon school will be out and the strawberries will be ripe and all the children from the village will be climbing the slopes to pick them. I shall want you to go with them so that we may have some of the delicious red berries too."

"But the babies can't eat strawberries," protested Marta.

"No, but the grandfather can. He suffers from thirst and complained only yesterday that the dry bread and cheese no longer satisfy him. But perhaps you can gather enough strawberries so that Peter's mother can make some of the good jams and jellies we all like so well. Then you will have pure air and bright sunshine and a chance to be of service too. Does that please you, Marta?"

"Yes, yes," cried the child with a happy little jump. "That pleases me very well."

By the time they reached home Marta had a bright bunch of flowers. She placed them on a bench in the garden beside the rose bushes which were not yet in bloom. Then, eagerly, she held out her arms to receive the pillow into which Martali had been carefully buttoned.

"Look! She's holding fast to my finger!" she cried, as she laid the baby on a blanket beside her brother.

Now Martali's eyes were open, wide and serious. Tobi was still fretting a little but soon he would be dozing off unaware that now he had a name of his own and a place in the village church.

"You see, Marta," the young mother said, "there is no cause to worry."

The Alm-Uncle, hearing Heidi's voice, called her to his room and stretched forth his hand, saying:

"Come, child, and tell your old grandfather about the service. How did the little ones behave? Was the church filled and did everything go as it should?"

Then Heidi related all the events of the morning while her grandfather listened intently, chuckling when she told him how Marta had spoken out during service and smiling as she described the christening.

"Someone tried to fill Marta's head full of superstitions about it," she added, "but I think I explained it so that she understood."

"She does not understand easily," the grandfather said, shaking his head. "Words mean nothing. She has to see things with her own eyes to understand them. She is not like you were, Heidi. These notions take hold of her strongly. You must explain things to her in pictures and that is most difficult— most difficult——"

His voice trailed off and he sat for a moment in silence. Then he asked:

"And what did the neighbours think? Were they pleased with the babies' names?"

"Andre was well pleased, Grandfather," Heidi answered, seating herself on the stool by his feet so that she might be near him while she talked. "He has promised to call on us this afternoon."

"Just like the old days," said the grandfather with a sigh. "His father often used to come up from Mels for a visit. He offered to teach your father the trade, and later, when he had sons of his own, we still saw each other occasionally. But then came the accident and the very word 'carpenter' became hateful to me. I was wrong, but my good friend died before I had a chance to tell him. The boys were brought to Dorfli by their mother, but now she is gone and even the brothers no longer see each other. Poor Andre is a lonely man."

"He must be very lonely," agreed Heidi, who was always deeply touched by other people's sorrows. "I often see him looking after his hut all by himself and wish I might make life more cheerful for him."

"And why not?" said the grandfather. "Welcome him like an old friend when he comes this afternoon, Heidi. Offer him bread and cheese and the best cakes and sausage. Let him feel that he is one of us, and if there is anything to be fixed, ask him to fix it. You will be needing a carpenter about when I am gone."

"But, Grandfather," protested Heidi, tears rushing to her eyes. "I cannot bear to think of such a thing. Surely you will be well again. You mustn't be saying such things. Why, you're going to stay with us a long time and watch Tobi and Martali grow to be big children——"

"Now, now," said the old man, placing his hand on her head. "You must try and see it as I do. At my age every day should be counted as a gift from God. And who am I that I should be left to enjoy His mercies when so many younger men have been taken? The doctor was much younger than I am.

And there was your poor father, crushed by a falling beam when he was barely twenty, and your lovely young mother who was already ill when he was brought home to her. The villagers all said she was too weak to stand trouble. But it was not the truth. She was a brave, courageous woman. She gave my son two years of such happiness as many people never know in an entire lifetime. But, like everything, it had to come to an end."

"What was she like, Grandfather?" Heidi asked after a moment. She had always wondered about her mother but hesitated to ask for fear of bringing the tragedy before her grandfather's eyes. But now he talked on and on, only pausing when he grew short of breath. His son had been the light of his life and he spoke of Adelheid with great affection. How different she must have been from her sister Dete who thought only of fine clothes and high wages! Thankfulness filled Heidi's heart as she listened. She had never admitted, even to herself, that vague fear that the sisters might have been alike. Now the grandfather's words showed her the mother who had died before she could remember her as the good woman she really was.

"Andre can tell you more about your parents if you care to hear it," the grandfather finished. "I would have spoken of this before but I do not talk readily of things that are close to my heart. Once I thought I should never find peace again but today when the church bells were ringing it came to me that at last I had found it. You and Peter are as happy as Adelheid and Tobias, and I have lived to see it. What more can I ask? What greater blessing could ever come to me?"

"Dear Grandfather," said Heidi, kissing his forehead, as she rose to leave him, "I shall not grieve you with tears again. But now you must rest or you will be too tired for Andre to visit. Shall I tidy your bed?"

He motioned her away with his hands, saying that he pre-
ferred to rest in his chair. Later, when she came in with his
dinner, she found him fast asleep and breathing regularly.
Covering the tray with a napkin, she left it beside him and was
about to tiptoe out of the room when she heard the carpenter's
voice outside:

"Well, here it is! As fine a little bed as these humble hands
could carve. Put the infants in at once and see how they like it."

"Andre!" cried Heidi, throwing open the door. "You've brought
us a gift. Look, Jamy! The most beautiful bed. It has a rail all
around it so that the babies can play in it and not fall out and I
do believe it just fits in that snug place behind the tiled stove
where my bed used to be."

"Well, let's try it," said the carpenter, striding in with the
beautifully carved bed on his back. "There she is. A perfect fit.
This is the exact place for it. Now let's have a look at the
infants."

"Do you think you can tell which is which?" asked Jamy
mischievously. "Heidi and my little sister can, but the rest of us
are always saying Tobi for Martali and Martali for Tobi. Once
even Peter confused them and put Tobi on Martali's pillow."

"I had taken off the pink bow—that's why," said Heidi,
laughing as she and Jamy showed the carpenter through the
house to the garden behind it where the babies, both wide
awake, lay kicking and cooing on their pillows. The warm sun
bathed their hands and bare feet with golden light but their
eyes were carefully shaded by an overhanging bush. Marta had
seen to that. She was there watching them.

"Well, little lady," the carpenter greeted her. "They tell me
you know them apart. Which is the boy and which is the girl?
Can you tell me so that I, too, will know them?"

"Of course I can," said Marta, looking important as she pointed out the baby on the first pillow. "This is Tobi. You see, his arms are a little stronger and his hair grows farther back on his head than Martali's. Her hair curls a little more, but their eyes are exactly the same. You could never tell them apart if you looked only at their eyes."

"Nor could you tell them from Adelheid," said the carpenter thoughtfully. "Heidi, I remember your mother well, although I couldn't have been more than six years old when I last saw her. She had those eyes—the same gentle blue. They were the colour of the blue harebells that she used to gather to fill the vase on the table. If only you could have named the little girl for Adelheid——"

He stopped speaking then. Marta's look stopped him. She stood before him like a soldier, her chin up, her eyes flashing.

"You know she couldn't have named an innocent baby Adelheid," she said. "It would be calling down an affliction. The neighbours said so."

"Marta! Marta!" exclaimed Heidi in distress. "Surely you misunderstood them. How could my mother's name call down an affliction on Martali?"

"Because she was a sleepwalker. They said so. And wouldn't it be terrible if Martali walked in her sleep?"

At this the carpenter suddenly threw back his head and laughed aloud. Jamy stared at him, afraid that he had suddenly lost his senses, while Marta seized one of the babies and rushed into the house.

"Marta! Marta!" Heidi called after her. "Where are you taking Martali?"

"Will you give an old man no peace?" shouted the grandfather from his room. "Must you continually call the child's name?"

"She's afraid I'll drop Martali," cried Marta breathlessly. "Here, take her. I'm sure she's safe with you."

And with that she deposited the baby, pillow and all, in the lap of the startled old man.

"Here! Here!" he exclaimed. "What is the noise about? What is happening?"

"He laughed at her. He did! He did!"

"Who laughed?" asked the grandfather. "And is there any sin in laughing?"

"Let me explain it," pleaded Heidi when she saw that Marta could not make herself understood. "Andre is here and I took him to see the babies first, because I thought you were sleeping. We were talking about their names and Marta told him Martali couldn't have been named for my mother because she was a sleepwalker. Well, Andre laughed. So far as I could see, that is all there was to it. He simply laughed because Martali will need to learn to walk before she can possibly walk in her sleep."

"Hm!" said the grandfather, stroking his chin. "So that's what they've been saying. Perhaps Andre knows more about this sleepwalking than you think. Call him in. Let's hear what kind of story he has to tell."

The carpenter was summoned. He looked a little sheepish as he came in with Jamy and Brigitte who also wanted to enjoy the visit and thank him for the gift he had brought.

"I never meant to frighten the child," he explained. "But her words called Adelheid to mind so clearly. The villagers used to wonder how it was that she managed to walk out of the house every evening after she was sent to bed. But I ask you, Uncle, how else would she ever have seen Tobias? I know from my father that her mother and sister Dete had forbidden her to see him."

"Thought the boy had as little sense as his father," the Alm-Uncle commented grimly. "But so long as Tobias looked after her Adelheid was well."

"Then she didn't really walk in her sleep?" questioned Marta, wide-eyed.

"She may have done so once or twice," the Alm-Uncle said. "Who can say for sure? But sleepwalking is no great affliction. Many people have walked in their sleep when their rest was disturbed or they were uneasy about something."

"I know that to be true," Heidi put in. "I did it at Frankfurt simply because I was homesick."

"There, you see," said the carpenter. "And now may I give the little lady a piece of advice? She has learned to use her eyes well. She can tell the babies apart better than anyone else. But she must still learn to tell the truth from gossip. Words are like the nails I use to build my houses. You can either hammer them straight or crooked. It all depends on the sort of house you are trying to build."

Marta had been listening to all this attentively. There was more in what the carpenter said than she could comprehend.

"But suppose I don't want to build a house?" she asked at length.

"Ah, but one has to," he replied.

"And suppose," asked the Alm-Uncle, leaning forward, "suppose one has driven in many crooked nails. Do you think, Andre, that it would be possible to go back and straighten them? To pull out a few and drive them in true and straight before that house was left for somebody else to live in?"

"I do, Uncle," he answered. "I most certainly do."

"Then if you will excuse us," the old man said as he motioned the others away, "Andre and I have a little nailing to do."

After about five minutes of listening outside the Alm-Uncle's door, Marta announced, "I don't hear any hammering."

"I do," said Heidi, putting her arm about the child and drawing her away from the door. "They're clearing up an old misunderstanding and the words they are saying are like the sound of a hammer. For many years my grandfather lived alone on the Alm. People in the village had spread unkind gossip about him saying that the accident to my father was the Lord's judgement and no more than he deserved. It seemed whenever there is an accident somebody has to blame somebody else. So, because the villagers blamed him, Grandfather blamed the carpenter, for it was he who had taught my father the trade."

"But it wasn't his fault," protested Marta, trying very hard to follow what Heidi was telling her.

"That's so," she replied. "It wasn't. Perhaps Grandfather is saying as much to Andre now. That is what he means by pulling out old nails and driving them in straight and true—-"

"I see it now!" cried the child. "That's the sound the good hammer makes—*Wahr! Wahr! Wahr!* But the bad hammer slips off the nail and says: *Gesch-watz! Gesch-watz!*"

"Good!" exclaimed Heidi, clapping her hands. "You've learned your lesson well." But to herself she thought, "Grandfather is right. She does have to see things in pictures before she understands them."

Chapter 9

Strawberry Time

*J*ust before school closed for the Summer Jamy received a letter from Paris:

Chère Jeanne-Marie:
Your mama and I hope that by now you have had enough of peasant life and are ready to return home. We have taken the old château in Vaud for the Summer and expect to do some entertaining. You will surely want to meet some of the guests we have invited. There is an interesting young scientist, Max Tauber, who has expressed the hope you will return. He has made a study of the geology of Switzerland and you might compare impressions as I am sure your passion for the country, like his, is only youthful fancy.

Jamy was reading the letter aloud, but here Heidi interrupted her to ask, "Could that be our Max? He is in Paris. He's taken Chel under his wing since the doctor died, but I didn't know he was a scientist. He's the son of the pastor here——"

"It couldn't be the same one then," Jamy decided quickly and went on with her letter.

As for Marta, let her stay if she is being benefited by the climate. I hardly see how she will fit into our plans in her present emotional state.

"What does that mean?" asked Marta. She had been sitting on the stove bench, elbows on knees, waiting for her name to be mentioned.

"Why, I believe you used to cry a great deal," said Jamy, smiling.

"But I don't now."

Jamy kissed her. "No, darling, you don't, and if I tell Papa that I'm sure he'll let you stay. As for this scientist—who wants to meet a dull old professor interested only in the geology of this country? What can I tell him of its beauty and its people?"

"You are welcome to stay as you planned, Jamy," Heidi reminded her.

"I know. I *know*. But, Heidi, do you know how long it has been since my father has written to me or even seemed to be aware of my existence? I can't disappoint him now. I shall probably have a miserable time but there is nothing else for me to do. You see that, don't you?"

Heidi considered the matter thoughtfully for a moment.

"Yes," she said at last, "I see that and a great deal more. For sometimes things work out quite differently than we expect. It may be the pastor's son and, if it is, you're sure to like him. Anyway, you will be able to look up Chel and find out how he is getting along with his art work. Then you'll meet Max, if you haven't already met him. You see, it's right for you to go to Paris and so it must be best. After all, it's only three months. You'll be back again to teach in the Autumn."

"Yes, surely I will be back," Jamy said, "and until then I can

be certain that Marta is in the best of hands. But I'll miss you
both——"

And then, before she should cry and disgrace herself in the
eyes of the little sister who had so bravely overcome her tears,
she rushed from the room to pack and be off lest she should
change her mind.

At first Marta seemed hardly aware of her sister's absence.
The day she left, three of her schoolmates—Erna, Nanni and
Germaine—came in with the news that strawberries were ripe
on the Alm.

"Please go with us," begged Erna. "I know a place where they
ripen first of all and Mama said I should ask you because you
never went strawberry picking before."

"How good you are!" exclaimed Marta. "You're right too. I
never have picked strawberries. When we lived in Vaud I was
too young and ever since then I've lived in big cities where you
buy them in little wooden crates. Heidi! Heidi!" she called.
"May I have a crate to put strawberries in?"

At this the others laughed and nudged one another. Then
Marta saw that they each carried two baskets which looked
more like upside-down straw hats than anything. These were
called *kratten* and fitted one inside the other. As they had no
covers Marta wondered how she could carry such baskets down
the steep slope without spilling some of the berries. She called
again to Heidi and this time her call was answered.

"Here are the baskets which I once used for picking," she
said, handing two of the hat-shaped *kratten* to Marta. "Now do
as the other children do and I am sure your first excursion to
the berry patch will be a pleasure for all of us."

"I will," Marta promised. And she started off with the others,

swinging her baskets gaily. But when they were partway up
the first slope, she thought of something.

"Aren't we going in the wrong direction?" she asked.
"Heidi said the strawberry patch was at the edge of the
glacier."

"Ours isn't," Erna replied. "It would take half the day to
climb to the edge of the nearest glacier. We pick just a little
way above on the sunniest slope."

"Oh," said Marta, disappointed. "Then I can't touch the
glacier."

"Who would want to do such a thing?" laughed Germaine.
"A glacier is dirty. You just ought to see how dirty it is. Far off
it looks all pearly white but when you're close by it's simply
covered with mud."

"You ought to know that," put in Nanni, who liked to show
her importance. She was the warden's daughter and, usually, no
one questioned her opinions.

"But I didn't," said Marta sadly. "I thought it would be
beautiful up there."

All her joy at picking the strawberries vanished and now
it seemed a long climb to the strawberry patch. There was
no path and often it was necessary to hold on to the rocks
above and swing up with great difficulty. Then would come
another grassy slope. Erna pointed out several places where
the strawberry plants grew thickly but on the first plants
the berries were very small and hard and green. A little
way higher up there were a few white ones. Then some had
pink cheeks and, at last, Nanni, who climbed more quickly
than the others, discovered one that was gleaming red and
fully ripe.

"Who finds the first
And eats it not,
Shall find the best
At another spot."

She sang out as she dropped it into her basket.

"Come on!" called Erna and Germaine, trooping after her. "There are sure to be whole stems full of ripe berries on the next slope."

Marta was a little behind. She had grown very tired and sat down to rest under a centaury bush that was covered with blossoms. How nice it would be, she thought, if she could simply pick the red flowers and fill her basket with those.

"Come on! Come on!" called Germaine from the slope above. "There are no ripe ones here but surely on the next slope——"

Marta had to continue. They climbed and climbed and finally she said, "Can't we go home if we don't find any on the next slope? I'm too tired to pick."

"But you can sit down once you find a good place. You can lie down and pick if you want to. Only wait! We'll go home with full baskets or, better yet, be finished in time to sell them in Maienfeld."

"Sell them!" exclaimed Marta. "Can little girls do that?"

"Certainly," returned Germaine. "Why not? I sell mine every summer. If I didn't I should have nothing to wear to school. Mama can't afford to buy me clothes but only food enough for us to eat."

"Will you all sell your berries?" questioned Marta, beginning to be puzzled.

"Certainly," they replied again and this time all three voices spoke at once.

"It is much better to sell them than to take them home," Nanni added. "You just see how pleased everybody will be if you sell your berries."

Marta was not at all sure of this but she remembered that Heidi had told her to do as the others did and so she supposed she must obey this command to the letter.

"All right," she said, "I'll sell mine too."

Now they had come to a steep cliff which rose up sheer and straight but at the side there was a jagged edge where, with great care, it might be possible to ascend.

"If there aren't any up there," Erna declared, "we might as well go home for this is the place I meant."

"Then let's look. Who wants to go first?"

Nobody seemed anxious to be first to try the jagged rocks and finally Erna, who was the tallest, had a plan.

"I'll hold Marta on my shoulders and she can look over and then if there aren't any berries there we won't bother to climb up."

This plan pleased everybody but Marta herself. She felt that Erna's shoulders were not nearly as safe a perch as the rocks might be. But once she was there she could really see the slope above. It looked as though a gay carpet had been thrown over it—a carpet with great rose patterns thickly spattered over the green.

"There aren't any berries," she called down, "but oh, such beautiful red flowers!"

"Are they centaury blossoms like those you saw before?" asked Nanni.

"Oh, no," Marta replied. "They're ever so much smaller plants and grow as thick as the crocus blossoms behind the church."

"Let me see them," coaxed Germaine, and Erna finally agreed. Germaine weighed even less than Marta for she seldom had enough to eat. She was boosted up as soon as Marta was safely landed on solid ground again. Now Germaine shaded her eyes and looked.

"Why, they're not flowers at all!" she exclaimed. "They're strawberries, but they're just as thick as Marta said. Now let me down!"

She was lowered with a bump but promptly scrambled after the others who were already climbing the jagged rocks. Marta was ahead as Nanni kept calling:

> *"You silly goose!*
> *You don't know strawberries!*
> *Would you know cheese?*
> *Would you know bread?*
> *Would you know dried apples?*
> *Would you know your own bed?"*

making a sort of chant of it which Germaine and Erna quickly learned and joined in singing.

Their voices were hateful to Marta. They thought it was fun to tease but if they had been new and she had been the one to call tantalising rhymes they would have hated it too. This is what she was thinking as she scrambled hastily up the rocks, without noticing whether or not she had a firm hold or a sure footing.

"Watch out!" called Erna suddenly, breaking off the song.

It was too late. Marta came tumbling down and the rock she had grasped tumbled after her. But on the jagged place below, her dress caught and saved her. The rock went skimming by, just missing her head and grazing Nanni's knee.

"There! See what you've done!" shrieked Nanni.

"She didn't mean it," the other two defended her.

Marta wanted desperately to cry. She felt sure the jagged rock had taken a piece out of her as well as her dress. But if she let these girls know she had hurt herself they would call her a goose again and probably start another song. Bravely she set her teeth together and picked herself up. Still she was ahead. But now she climbed more cautiously and when, at last, she did reach the top she was glad to sit down and simply reach out at either side to pick the wonderful red berries.

They were wild strawberries and therefore much sweeter than those one bought in the city shops. Marta tasted a few but then she saw that tasting them put her behind and picked all the faster. There was no crowding or pushing as is usually the case with strawberry pickers. Here there were enough to fill all the baskets and more besides. Not until the first baskets were filled did the girls stop to eat a few with the bread and cheese they had brought in their pockets.

When they were ready to leave Marta watched how Erna spread a large green leaf over her berries to keep them fresh and than fastened it down with sticks. She did the same, not asking, just watching and seeing how it was done.

"You learn quickly," said Nanni and this word of praise worked like a charm. All Marta desired now was to do as her friends did so that they would be pleased with her.

The sun was still high in the sky and the baskets were full.

"There will surely be time to sell them," Erna exclaimed as

they started down the hillside. "Hurry, Marta! Hurry, Nanni! Hurry, Germaine! My father is driving down to Maienfeld this afternoon, and if we hurry fast enough, we may be in time to ride down in the wagon with him."

Chapter 10

A Lesson in Values

When Marta started off for the strawberry patch that morning Heidi watched her with a happy heart. One of the delights of her own childhood had been berry picking and now this child, who was almost as dear to her as Tobi or Martali, would have the same pleasure. Not only that, but the strawberries would taste delicious with clabbered milk or cream. If any were left over she could begin to make the jellies and jams which she would store on the shelves in the cellar for a Winter treat.

Heidi, who had once been as happy as the little birds in the trees as she frolicked in the green meadows, was now as happy as a mother bird on her nest. Home became dearer and dearer to her as she went about her familiar, homely tasks.

As soon as Tobi and Martali were bathed and dressed she bundled their clothes under her arm and carried them to the fountain where there were always other housewives with their bundles to be washed. Then followed an hour of splashing and scrubbing and friendly chatter.

This morning the hard-working mother of Germaine Grube was there with a bundle several times as large as Heidi's, for her children went up like steps from the smallest, just learning to walk, to Germaine's older brother who already had work in the fields.

"Today begins the strawberry picking," she announced as she put down her bundle. "More berries, more clothes, more washing. That's how it goes. But the young ones must be dressed and if they earn it they will spend it. That's how it goes."

Heidi did not share Frau Grube's gloomy outlook but she could easily understand it.

"All this berry picking without a berry brought home," the woman went on in her monotonous, complaining voice. "It will be just as it was last year. New clothes for school, a fine new looking-glass. Where does Germaine get these high ideas? Is it from Erna whose father has two fine cows? Is it from Nanni, the warden's daughter? Or is it from the schoolmistress' sister? I tell her she should choose friends who have as little as she has and then she will not crave possessions beyond our means. Now what do you think she tells me?"

Wringing one of Germaine's dresses vigorously, she turned to Heidi.

"I can't imagine. What?"

"That she wants to be a schoolmistress and take Mamselle Jamy's place when she gets married."

"But what makes her think Jamy is going to get married?" asked Heidi again.

"She's pretty, isn't she?" Frau Grube made a wry face as though this were a misfortune. "Germaine is pretty too, if I am her mother and if I do say it, I that shouldn't——"

"But why shouldn't you?" laughed Heidi. "We all know that Germaine is both pretty and clever. She has a real love for her school books. So why shouldn't she become a teacher?"

"How can I send her to a fine school?" the mother asked hopelessly. "Me? I got along without such an education. Why can't Germaine be satisfied?"

"Thank the good Lord that she wants to better herself," put in the dressmaker, who had just arrived with several pieces of lace which she had finished and wished to wash before offering them for sale. "It pleases me to see a young girl take pride in her clothes. There's Marta, for instance, with never a curl out of place——"

"She was brought up to it. But look at my Lisi," sighed the old weaver woman. "There was a beautiful girl who could have had everything, but what happens? She works herself nearly to death to support a lazy husband. Yes, and she, too, wanted to better herself. What I say is, be content with what the Lord sends and He will send still more. Look at Heidi. Did she ever try to better herself? Not if my old eyes can still see what is happening. She has always been contented and what comes of it? The finest house in the village and two such handsome babies as a king might envy. Ah, me! The Lord knows best."

Heidi walked home a little saddened by the conversation over the fountain. She would have been just as happy on the Alm as in the great manor house. But, with the grandfather's illness, she had given up all thought of going up this Summer. Brigitte had grown heavy and could hardly climb the steep mountain path, and Heidi, who had always cherished a great respect for older people, felt that Tobi and Martali needed their grandmother's care fully as much as they needed hers.

But next Summer Peter would have his cows, and perhaps, as he added to his herd, he might give work to many of the poorer families of the village. Cheese making on a large scale would require several helpers. Then they could all go up to the Alm . . .

But could they? Or would it be only Peter and his helpers who would go?

"Where are your songs today?" asked the grandfather after Heidi had returned and had finished hanging the clean clothes. Usually she sang over her cleaning and polishing.

"I've been thinking about the poor people," she replied. "So many of them are unhappy."

The old man looked at her sharply. "Well, and what about the rich people—those who have large estates and lands and fine clothes. Are many of them happy?"

"No," she agreed, thinking of Jamy's family, "I'm afraid they're not."

"So, rich or poor, they find cause for complaint. And what can be done about it? They are afraid, like our little Marta. I know. For years, I, too, was afraid and no peace or happiness came to me. I tell you, Heidi, it's all in here." And he beat his hand upon his chest.

"You aren't afraid any more, are you, Grandfather?" Heidi asked.

"Not for myself," he answered, "and not for you or for the infants, as they are in good care. But for the child, yes. She is like a lost kid bleating for its mother. She is like Tolpet, the foolish one, and will continue to lose her way until she finds her place in the flock. The grandmother learned her lesson and did what she could but, I tell you, fear was born in the child. She must see her path clearly." He sighed deeply. "If only I could live to show it to her."   his wife

Heidi knew the grandfather was failing, as now he often spoke of dying and many times during the day he called for water. Today, it seemed, he called more often than usual as Marta was not there to run to the fountain.

When noontime came, Heidi helped him to the table. The short walk from his own room to the kitchen tired him now.

"Where's the child?" he asked, looking across at her empty place.

"She's gone for strawberries——"

"Ah, they will keep me from being so thirsty. I believe I will have only the goats' milk now and wait for the strawberries. But can she find them? Did the child go alone?"

"No, indeed," Heidi replied. "Three of her schoolmates called for her and she went with them. Erna said the berries were ripe so I packed a little bread and cheese——"

"Did you put in any dried apple?" Brigitte interrupted. "She is especially fond of it."

"And sausage?" questioned Peter, helping himself to a large piece as he spoke.

"You're spoiling the child," declared the Alm-Uncle severely. "If she carried such a fine lunch to the berry patch, how will her schoolmates feel who cannot afford as much?"

"You're right, Grandfather," agreed Heidi, thankful that she had given Marta only bread and cheese.

The clatter of dishes being cleared away after a meal was always a pleasing sound to the Alm-Uncle's ears. He slept for a little while, but late in the afternoon he sat up straight in his chair and called to Heidi in a loud voice:

"The child should be home by now! Such a delicate one cannot stand it all day in the sun. If there are any berries, surely by now she has picked them."

"Don't worry, Grandfather," Heidi told him. "See, the sun is still high in the sky——"

"But when it comes in the west windows and reflects on the

mirror there—see how it does! Then I know it is growing late. Look at the wall clock. It is now nearly five."

A few moments later Heidi heard the clock striking. The grandfather rarely looked at it or at the heavy gold watch he carried in his pocket, for the sun told him the time with greater accuracy.

"Where did they go?" he called out again. "Did the children tell you where they expected to find these early strawberries?"

"I believe it was on the slope," Heidi reassured him.

"But suppose they have gone as far as the precipice——"

"They wouldn't, Grandfather. They don't know the way."

"But suppose they have tried to find the way and the child has wandered off! She would not look ahead so long as the ground at her feet was solid. I tell you, Heidi, she knows only what she sees."

Never had Heidi seen the grandfather more anxious. As the hours passed and the sun sank lower and lower he rose from his chair and began pacing from window to window.

"This will be the undoing of him," exclaimed Brigitte in alarm when she saw it. "If Peter would come home we could send him to look for the children."

"I'll go," volunteered Heidi, handing Martali to her grandmother, for the baby, also, had been fretting for Marta.

She ran at once to Barbel's house. Perhaps Erna had returned with news of the berry pickers. But no one was there; the door was closed and everything still. Then a neighbour told her she had seen their wagon pass by on the way to Maienfeld a few hours before.

"Were there any children in it?" Heidi asked eagerly.

The neighbour shook her head. She had seen only Dame

Barbel and her husband on the front seat. The children might have been in the back. She couldn't say.

Heidi ran on to the warden's house but he was also out. She would get no news from Nanni. Then she tried Frau Grube's ancient black chalet as she could not return to the grandfather with no news whatsoever. Here the children crowded to the door, all talking at once.

"She's gone——"

"She's not either. She's just out."

"She's down in the goat-shed——"

At last Heidi gathered that it was their mother, and not Germaine, about whom they were talking. She ran down to the shed and there she got some information. Frau Grube was standing inside spreading clean straw for the goats which provided her large family with milk. When questioned she said she had heard Germaine call out something about selling her berries from a wagon that was passing. No, she had not seen Marta in the wagon. She had not seen Germaine, for that matter. She had only heard her call as the wagon rumbled by.

At last, after two weary hours, Heidi came back. But she was alone. To the grandfather's anxious questions she could only reply that she had no word of Marta. One of the children had returned to sell her berries and that was all she knew.

"But perhaps Marta could not keep up with the others and stayed on to fill her baskets——"

"But it is already dark," quavered the old man. "She could not see to pick berries in the dark."

Just then a step sounded outside. It was Peter returning late from the fields. He had borrowed a lantern from the man he was helping.

"I will get together a party of men at once," he promised.

"Andre is home and the pastor's youngest son will go with me——"

He broke off, opening his eyes in surprise as a happy song floated up to him from somewhere farther down in the village:

> "Strawberry time! Strawberry time!
> Up the mountainside we climb;
> We filled the baskets with berries
> On their stems as large as cherries;
> On the top the leaves we pressed;
> Mine were best! Mine were best!"

"It's Marta's voice!" exclaimed the Alm-Uncle, drawing a great breath of relief. "Thank God, it's Marta!"

"You see, nothing happened," said Heidi, turning with a smile. "They're coming with berries. I suppose they just lingered as children do."

"The berries will taste good," replied the grandfather, sitting back exhausted from his long hours of anxiety.

The lantern Peter was holding threw its light far out across the steps as Heidi held back the door. Marta came up, swinging her baskets.

"Let me see the berries. I heard you singing our old strawberry song!"

"Yes, yes," called the Alm-Uncle. "Come in at once and let us all have a look at the fine berries you have gathered."

"But—but——" Marta began.

"Never mind showing us now," Peter said, lowering the light. "Go in at once to the uncle. He has been waiting for you all day."

Marta ran in but something clinked against the side of her basket as she ran.

"Look!" she exclaimed, holding up a shining coin. "I haven't any berries, but I have this instead. The children said you would be pleased. They said it was better to sell your berries and we all had a chance to ride down to Maienfeld. They said that children never brought their berries home if they could possibly sell them and mine really were best and I got the largest coin——"

She stopped, out of breath, but already she could see that her coin did not please the Alm-Uncle as a basket of glowing red berries would have done.

For a moment no one said a single word.

Then the Alm-Uncle burst out, as though there had been a great explosion in the room:

"So that is what you think? Child of your grandmother! Child of the aristocrats! You send her for berries and she brings home a coin! Bite it, child, and see if you get any flavour out of it. Set your teeth into it hard. That's it. How does it taste?"

Marta made a wry face but did as she was told.

"It tastes horrible," she said, her lip quivering.

"Of course it tastes horrible," shouted the Alm-Uncle, and his face grew very red in his excitement. "What can it buy as sweet as the berries you have sold? What can it buy, I say? What can a thousand coins buy if a man is thirsty and has no water? I tell you, child, until you have learned that there are some things more precious than silver coins you have learned nothing."

"Don't mind him too much," said Heidi gently, putting an arm about Marta's trembling shoulder. "He's been worse today and he suffers from thirst. All day long he's had nothing but goats' milk, waiting for the berries which would be juicy and sweet——"

"Well, tomorrow he shall have them," said Marta, lifting her chin. "I'll fill my baskets to the very top tomorrow in the same place and not taste a single one, and if I should be offered a coin for every berry I would not sell them. But you told me to do as the other children did—and so I did."

"So that was it?" the Alm-Uncle asked huskily. "It was not your idea to sell the berries? You simply did as the others did?"

"Yes, that was it, and please forgive me," begged Marta, throwing herself on her knees beside him and beginning to sob aloud. "I didn't know you wanted the berries so. I never dreamed they tasted so wonderful until I bit that horrid coin. Oh, please forgive me! Please! Please!" And she beat her little fists on the stool and sobbed still harder. "Dear Lord, please forgive me if the Alm-Uncle won't."

"Dear Lord, forgive me," murmured the old man and he let his hand rest lovingly on her tangled curly head.

Chapter 11

When the Roses Bloomed

*A*ll during the sunny month of June Marta went strawberry picking almost every day. She forgot her anxiety for Martali in her efforts to please the Alm-Uncle and it was to him she ran first with her berries. She seldom ate any out of the basket for she felt they were all his, and in the evening she often sang to him or told him stories of her life with her grandmother or, later, with her mama and papa. But he seemed most interested when she talked of the grandmother.

Jamy wrote, saying that the young scientist was indeed the pastor's son and her letters were full of praise for Chel and the young man who liked to call himself Chel's Uncle Max. She found her mama's parties much more entertaining than she had remembered them to be and added, especially for Marta, "When you grow up you will want to come to Paris too. So hurry and become a fine lady. Mama will like you better if you call her Marie. I do and it makes a great difference."

"What's the use of having a mama if you can't call her that?" asked Marta, perplexed.

"You may call me mama if you like," said Heidi, half in fun. But Marta took it seriously and asked:

"May I really? And will you really love me like a mama?"

"I do already, precious girl," Heidi replied, holding her very close.

"If I could just stay here forever," sighed Marta, for the thought that one day things would change and she would have to leave weighed heavily upon her heart. Jamy's letters suggested the possibility that she might fall in love with this stranger called Max, and if that happened Marta thought she would surely be sent back to Paris to the woman who wanted to be called Marie, instead of mama, and the papa who seldom noticed her.

Here she was surrounded by love. Peter, Heidi and Brigitte all treated her as though she belonged to the family. The babies cooed and smiled when she came near them, and the Alm-Uncle hardly let an hour pass without calling for her. Besides, there were the long sunny hours in the strawberry patch more delightful than anything Marta had ever known. When the slopes were picked over there were still shady places in the cool forest below where strawberries still larger and more delicious than the others grew in abundance.

On her way home from these excursions Marta also brought flowers for the table. Sometimes when she found a rare plant that she knew Heidi would like, she dug it up with a sharp stone and carried it home to be set out in the garden. July had come and the garden was filled with roses. The bushes were covered with buds and everywhere windows were opened wide. It was truly a year of roses.

Just outside the kitchen window, where roses nodded down from the window boxes and the vine along the wall of the garden, Tobi and Martali were sleeping on their pillows. Their little round arms were thrown out as though they had been trying to fight off sleep and their hands were opened like petals.

Brigitte sat nearby with her knitting and Heidi was busy in a far corner of the garden snipping off a few dead roses so that the new buds might open more fully. But every now and then she laid down her scissors and went in to make sure the grandfather was comfortable. For several days he had not gone to his bed at night, but had continued sitting in his place by the window where the perfumed air fanned his face and where he could see the purple of evening deepening over the village, and then the stars.

"This is the last time I shall see the roses blooming in Dorfli," he explained when Heidi urged him to leave the window and rest a little. "Soon I shall rest, but first there are a few things I want you to do."

He took up a square paper which he had managed to remove from a nearby drawer where he kept his personal treasures.

"Take care of this," he said. "Chel painted it, and now that he is studying in Paris it is well for you to keep it to remember him. Perhaps to remember me."

The painting was an exact likeness of the grandfather just as he used to sit on his bench outside the Alm hut. It had been sketched first in charcoal and then painted in water colours, giving a lifelike tint to everything—the neighbouring Alps, the tall fir trees, the rust-red alpine roses. There was even a healthy glow on the cheeks of the old man himself. Comparing them Heidi saw that the grandfather's face was much whiter than the face in the picture.

"Grandfather," she asked anxiously, "are you sure you should be moving about so much today when only yesterday you were so weak?"

"The Lord has given me strength," he said, "but soon the time will come for me to leave you, and when one is about to make a long journey, one must be prepared."

"But we need you!" cried Heidi. "We're not ready to have you go just yet, Grandfather——"

"Ah, no," he answered. "My work is done. The child is contented here and you and Peter are young and strong. You have many years ahead of you. Use them to make others happy. Use them more wisely than I have used mine. Have nothing to regret when the end comes—no crooked nails to be straightened——"

But at this the old man faltered and could not go on. The long speech had exhausted him and it was several moments before he spoke again. Then he asked to be moved a little nearer the window where he could breathe more easily.

The passing of the good doctor from Frankfurt had left Dorfli without a physician. Heidi considered sending to Maienfeld, but the grandfather urged her not to think of it.

"No doctor can cure old age," he said. "Only the Lord can cure it in His own good time."

"But the pain, Grandfather——"

"There is no pain." He paused, finding it difficult to breathe. "I am only very tired."

"But if you lay down on your bed, wouldn't that rest you, Grandfather?"

"That I cannot do," declared the old man. "I tell you, I must be prepared. I must straighten a few nails, as the carpenter said."

"But everything is straight," Heidi told him. "You've been a good grandfather. You've been everything to me—everything.

You've been father and mother and grandfather all in one. There is no one like you. No one at all."

"I'm leaving you very little, Heidi," he said sadly, "only the hut and few acres on the Alm. Peter can pasture his cows there and perhaps turn my workshop into a cheese-room. The shelves would be right for drying cheese and the presses and copper kettles are all there. Tell him they're all his—and now another thing. I've kept this in my watch case long enough. You may as well take the whole watch. Time is of no use to an old man."

And he laid in her hand his own beautiful watch, the one she had admired ever since she had first come to live with him. Now the case was open. She had never known before that it was meant to open. But, all this time, her grandfather had been saving a lock of someone's hair. She touched it. Silk could have been no softer. It was the colour of ripe chestnuts and curled a little at the end.

"Whose is it, Grandfather?" she asked wonderingly.

"My wife's. I thought you ought to have it. And now there's just one thing more. I have something to give the child. There it is." He indicated a square package beside the picture. "Her cross is broken. This ought to fix it. But now I have talked enough. Water, little one! Heidi, send the child for water."

Marta's hand trembled as she carried the mug back from the fountain. She knew the Alm-Uncle must be worse, but it pleased her to be allowed to wait on him. His voice was low and very gentle as she held out the water.

"Marta," he said, calling her directly by name for the first time. "Marta, I knew you would come back. Now I'm ready to forgive you——"

Marta raised questioning eyes to Heidi.

"It's all right, dear. You haven't done anything wrong. He's very ill. He doesn't know what he's saying."

"Water!" he called again.

He only sipped a little and then closed his eyes. Marta, thinking that now he must surely rest, ran back to the garden where the babies were sleeping.

"I'll mind them now if you want to go in to the uncle," she told Brigitte and the woman promptly put down her knitting and hurried inside.

The garden had walls around it which were partly crumbled away and in the centre were tiles with short grass growing between them. Once this place had been a chapel of the great manor house but, since the roof had fallen entirely away, Heidi transformed it into what Marta liked to call her fairyland. All around the edges were rose bushes of every description, now fully in bloom. A few star flowers looked up, like bright jewels set along the ancient tiles, and there were many clusters of fragrant garden violets.

Marta sat down beside Martali's pillow, thinking how like a rose she looked as she slept. Flowers were all around her. Now the fragrance came up almost as though they were breathing on her face. In the cities where Marta had lived there had been nothing like this. The tiles could be the roofs of a fairy village and the grass between, the trees. Poking her finger underneath, she managed to loosen a tile and, as she turned it back, tiny beetles with many legs scurried away as this had been their home.

"I'm a giant to them," thought Marta. "It's just the same as it would be if a big hand lifted the roof of this house and carried it away."

She looked up and suddenly realized that the garden was

really part of the house and that it had once had a roof.
Something really had lifted it—some mighty force that she
found it hard to understand. As she puzzled over it the picture
she had formed in her mind became more real to her. Above,
the clouds were like fingers across the sky. Her thoughts whirled
faster. Suppose the hand should come down! down! Why, she
would be as helpless as those poor beetles whose home she had
lifted from over their heads. She glanced at the clouds again;
then she looked at the babies. Suddenly both of them were
wide awake as though they too had seen the reaching hand.
Martali began to cry. Marta looked about for something to
comfort her and then ran in to ask Heidi if she might have the
large gourd which she used for a rattle.

"Martali's awake," she announced, "and she's fretting a little. Maybe she's ready to play and if I had the gourd I could
shake it for her. She always laughs when she hears the seeds
rattling inside and I'll be glad to do it——"

She stopped, her voice sounding suddenly loud in the still
room. The Alm-Uncle was no longer in the chair by the
window, but was lying on his bed with his eyes closed and an
expression of peace and contentment on his white face.

"Oh, I didn't mean to speak out. I didn't mean to wake
him."

"You won't wake him, dearest Marta," said Heidi.

"I suppose he was tired from sitting in the chair so long. But
he must feel better or he wouldn't have gone to sleep."

"He does feel better," said Heidi, tears rushing to her eyes
although she tried to smile to comfort the child. "He feels so
very much better, darling. I'm sure he wouldn't want us to be
sad."

"Oh!" said Marta. "Oh! Oh!"

For now the truth became clear to her. But still she could not believe it. He had been sitting there sipping the water she had brought; then she had gone out in the garden and while she was there a hand had reached down and taken him. She remembered the cloud and how she had lifted the stone. Suddenly it all seemed too terrible and she began to scream and sob, rushing from the room and out into the garden where she threw herself on the grass and sobbed until she was exhausted. Then she fell asleep.

Heidi found her there, all limp and tear-stained, and realised that she must forget her own grief and try to comfort this child to whom death was so strange. She must make her see how the grandfather had only passed over the borderland into that other garden, still more beautiful than the one on earth, and how he had been looking forward to his journey.

Two lines from a half-forgotten hymn came to Heidi's mind and, as they brought such peace to her, perhaps Marta would understand when she heard that——

> *"Even Death is not Unkind*
> *When Living Love is left behind."*

Chapter 12

The House on a Rock

*T*he days that followed were difficult ones for both Heidi and Marta. Nothing that she could do or say comforted the child, for always that picture of the reaching hand was before her eyes and she was filled with fear.

"It's always like this when I love someone," she sobbed. "Something must have happened at my christening too, for whenever I love anybody so much that I think I can't live another day without him, the Lord takes him away. It was like this with Grandma and now the Alm-Uncle. Oh, it would have been better if I had kept on hating him! I cannot bear it! I cannot! I cannot!"

And Marta sobbed as if nothing could ever make her stop while Heidi sat patiently beside her, waiting until the storm was spent. Then she said softly:

"Dearest Marta, if I felt as you do, I could not bear it either. But with faith one accepts what must be and even though we can no longer see our loved ones we know they are not lost to us, for Love is stronger than Death. So, you see, it would not have been better if you had hated the dear uncle for then you would not have this beautiful memory."

These words cheered Marta a little, but Heidi knew very well that all was not yet clear to her. But perhaps the Alm-Uncle had foreseen this and left something in the square package which would be more of a comfort. When her sobs had subsided, Heidi brought it out.

"It was his present to you, dear," she said. "Open it carefully for I'm sure he has given you something precious."

"Oh!" said Marta, taking the package. "May I open it in the garden? That's where I was when——"

"Of course you may," Heidi said quickly. "Run along with it, dear. I know you want to open it by yourself."

Marta undid the wrappings eagerly, for surely, if the Alm-Uncle had given it to her, it would be something with value greater than any coin. That was the sort of present he would give. Something that would make everything clear. Would she ever again, she wondered, understand her history as well as when he explained it? When school opened again, who would help her with those difficult lessons so that they were all as clear as day?

The first wrapping fell off the package and fluttered to the ground. Still there was another and another. It must be a very small present for now she was down to the third wrapper and nothing appeared but another square of folded paper. She shook it out. Yes, it was the last. But nothing was written on the paper. Nothing at all.

Perplexed, Marta stood there in the garden wondering what was meant by this sort of present. Surely it meant something, just as the pieces of dried apple had. It was something she was supposed to understand. Then, like a flash, she knew.

She had run out to the garden eager, expectant. She had opened the paper and found nothing. That, in itself, was a lesson. Everything that happened was like that. You looked at a glacier from a distance and it was beautiful, but close by it was muddy and dirty, as Germaine had said. Everything was less than you expected. Everything? Everything!

Now Marta's tears fell afresh and she threw herself on the ground underneath the rose bushes and kicked and beat her fists in her disappointment and anguish. A few petals fell, as though the roses were weeping with her, and Heidi ran out to see what had caused this new outburst of tears.

"It wasn't anything," Marta repeated over and over when first Heidi and then Peter and Brigitte questioned her about her present.

"But surely it must have been," Heidi insisted. "He wouldn't have given you an empty paper."

"But he did! He did! Look for yourself!"

"I can't believe it!" exclaimed Heidi, searching frantically through the scattered papers. "He wouldn't do a thing like that. He'd give you something to make you happy, Marta. He'd have to. That's the kind of person he was."

Marta only shook her head and sobbed still louder.

"It didn't make me happy to bite the coin, did it? He just wanted to teach me not to expect anything—ever—and now I won't."

Heidi, who had unbounded faith in the Alm-Uncle's goodness, could not believe any such thing as this.

"Peter, what shall we do?" she cried, appealing to her husband.

"Just keep on looking," he returned determinedly. "There must have been something. She may have let it fall out by accident."

So Peter and Heidi both searched and Brigitte helped by sweeping everything clean and going through the dustpan so

thoroughly that nothing could have escaped her. It was true.
There was nothing lying about in the whole garden except one
small tile which Peter put back in its place.

"Well," said Brigitte calmly, placing her hands on her hips,
"it seems there's nothing left for us to do but pray."

"You're right, Mother," agreed Peter. "Heidi, bring your
violin and we'll all sing Marta's prayer. I could use a little faith
and strength myself."

"But I don't want to," suddenly screamed out Marta. "I don't
want to pray to a God who takes away everything I love. Next
thing it will be Martali. And even if we pray and pray and beg
Him not to, it won't make any difference because He's up there
watching like an eagle and it's always the dearest one that He
takes away."

"How can you say such a thing?" cried Heidi, close to tears
herself as she picked up the baby girl for a reassuring hug.

"But He will——"

"Hush!" commanded Brigitte in a firm voice. "Not another
word of such blasphemy. If you will not pray, then we'll all pray
for you, that the Lord will make your heart clean and let no
more words like those come from your lips."

Marta was now frightened out of her sobbing. Heidi followed
the others into the house with a heavy heart, for it grieved her
to see the child so lost and bewildered. She had seen nothing
with her eyes that would make her accept God as a loving
father. But what could one see? Heidi tried to remember how
she had learned to trust in God and believe everything was for
the best. This trust had come to her as easily as her own breath
up on the Alm. But in Frankfurt it had been more difficult.
There she had learned from a book filled with beautiful pictures. These stories from the Bible were still in the bookcase,

well worn to be sure, but always they had been carefully and lovingly handled. That evening Heidi brought out the treasured book and while she was turning the pages Marta came and sat beside her.

"Look!" she exclaimed, suddenly pointing. "There's a picture of the wind."

Heidi had never seen a picture of the wind in her book. Now she looked closely to discover what had caused this exclamation and, to be sure, there was a picture of the wind whistling and blowing about a frail house on a lonely beach. She had always thought of it as a house on the sand, but to Marta it was the wind.

"Read it to me," she now coaxed.

So, while she sat on the bench beside her looking at the pictures, Heidi read the story of the wise man who built his house upon a rock:

"And the rain descended, and the floods came,
and beat upon that house; and it fell not: for
it was founded upon a rock."

Then the story went on to tell of a foolish man who also built a house, not on a rock, but on the shifting sand:

"And the rain descended, and the floods came,
and the winds blew, and beat upon that house;
and it fell; and great was the fall thereof."

"That's like the story the carpenter told, isn't it?" asked Marta. "But what was the rock?"

"I think it must have been Faith," said Heidi, "for this man heard the words of another carpenter who said, 'Love one another' and with faith in this rule, he was able to live a good and noble life."

"You live by that rule too, don't you?" asked the child, looking up into Heidi's face.

"I try to, dear."

"Then this house is built on a rock too, isn't it? It won't fall down like that house in the picture of the wind? It's like this."

And she put her finger down on the picture of a rock with a strong house standing upon it.

Chapter 13

The Return of Jamy

*T*hat night Marta slept soundly, comforted by the thought that the house where she lived was built on the firm rock of Heidi's faith. But the garden and the beautiful slopes beyond it and the majestic snowy peaks gave her no such sense of security. When the clouds blew across the sky and appeared in wondrous forms, she imagined them waiting to spring upon Martali if she should be left for a moment unguarded.

Thus the Summer passed and soon it was time for lessons to begin again. Jamy returned and with her came the pastor's son; these two had eyes only for each other and young Max stayed on and on, prolonging his visit with his parents.

"They are a fine couple," said Brigitte, nodding wisely. "But isn't it strange that Jamy should have to go to Paris to meet a young man who was brought up not a mile from this door?"

Max and Jamy took long trips after school and on Saturdays and it was suspected that they talked of many things other than the geological structure of the rocks. Jamy always came home from these walks with sparkling eyes, never noticing that the eyes of her little sister were clouded with a fear that had not been there when she left her.

Although Max was a likeable young man with an almost
unbounded knowledge of nature and its many wonders, Marta
avoided him as if he had the smallpox and when, several weeks
after his arrival in Dorfli, he was called away on a scientific
expedition, she had hardly spoken two words to him. But
scarcely was he out of the house, after bidding Jamy good-bye,
than Marta turned upon her like a whirlwind.

"You're in love with him, aren't you?" she demanded.

"Why, of course not——" Jamy began.

"Then what are you blushing for? And why did you let him
kiss you? You are in love with him! You are! You are! And
you're going to marry him and then I'll have to leave this house
and go back to Mama and call her Marie and I shall hate that.
I'll never, never do it. I'd rather *die*! I'd rather *die*!"

And poor Marta kept repeating this, her voice rising to an
hysterical scream. Finally she threw herself on the stove bench,
striking her head against the tiles. But she was already screaming so loudly that no one could tell whether she had felt the
bump or not.

Jamy turned to Heidi in dismay.

"What has happened? What has come over her? She hasn't
had a screaming spell for such a long time and I told Marie that
she was all over them——"

"She's not Marie! And I won't go back!" came from the
stove bench in hysterical sobs.

"Come, Jamy, leave her by herself until she's quietened down
a little," said Heidi, taking her friend's arm and walking with
her to the garden where an early frost had dressed everything in
the red and gold splendour of Autumn.

From the garden they could hear the sobs growing less and
less until they ceased altogether, and Heidi, peeping cautiously

into the living-room, discovered that Marta had sobbed herself to sleep.

"Now tell me what has happened," urged Jamy when Heidi had returned and the two of them were sitting on a bench in the shade of the gold-leaved beech tree just outside the wall.

"It's a long story," began Heidi. "A great deal has happened since you left early in June. At first Marta was as happy and healthy as a young kid and spent nearly every day picking strawberries. But then Grandfather died and everything changed——"

"Then Mama was right," sighed Jamy. "When you wrote and told us about it she said, 'The poor little thing, up there without her family and a death in the house! I really should have had your father send for her too!' But I know how helpless she is once Marta begins screaming and so I told her the passing of the Alm-Uncle would not affect her as much as she feared for the child was not very fond of him——"

"But she was, Jamy," Heidi interrupted. "Even before you left, she had begun to depend on him for help with her lessons. Then he became weaker and I sent her for strawberries, but she didn't realise I wanted them for him and sold them. He became quite furious with her, making her bite the coin she had received to prove to her that there was no sweetness in it."

"How like her grandmother!" exclaimed Jamy. "The poor woman spent hours with both of us trying to convince us that money was the root of all evil. Probably that's why the Alm-Uncle's lesson went home."

"No doubt it was," agreed Heidi, pausing to throw a shawl over her shoulders as the air was growing colder. "But from then on, Jamy, she couldn't do enough for Grandfather. She was with him almost constantly and when he died she had the

first one of these terrible crying spells. They've been repeated at
intervals ever since. And the sad part of it is, she finds no
comfort in the dear Lord, but blames Him for taking away first
her grandmother and then the uncle whom she had learned to
love as though he were her own grandfather."

"It's very sad," said Jamy with a sigh. "But what can be
done? Marta needs someone to depend on. Perhaps now she
will learn to depend on you."

"That's the thing I'm most afraid of," said Heidi. "She
mustn't. For it is true, she won't always be here with me and
she can't go through life depending on others, and never on
herself. Do you know, I think your grandmother must have
realised this when she taught her that lovely prayer?"

"I'm sure she did," Jamy agreed. "Our grandmother was a
noble woman, but she was like Marta. The thing I'm afraid of is
that poor Marta will have to learn her lesson through suffering,
as Grandmother did. She depended on others too. She depended on her parents who were rich and gave her everything
she desired. Then she fell in love with a soldier who married
her and tried to make her happy. The family was not pleased
with this marriage and refused to help the young couple. Grandmother soon found she couldn't live without all the luxuries to
which she had been accustomed. She left her husband, after he
had spent his last sou trying to provide for her and broken his
spirit as well, and returned home with my father, who was only
a baby. There was another child, a little older, who refused to
leave his father. So, you see, her family was divided and a short
time afterwards her parents died and left her with nothing but
the money which had seemed so important to her. She tried to
depend on that, but it never brought her happiness."

"And did she never see her husband and older son again?" asked Heidi.

"No, never," Jamy replied. "They were very bitter against her—and no wonder. She came to understand that the trouble was all her fault for placing such a great value on money and what it buys, and so small a value on love. Years later, she heard the prayer you spoke of sung at a church service in Budapest. She told me all this and begged me never to let Marta forget the hymn, for it was when she heard the words:

'Dear Spirit, dwell in me'

that she first realized where she could find someone who would never fail her. From then on she devoted her whole life to Marta and me. She tried to teach us all she had learned through her long years of suffering, but Marta was too young. She's named for grandmother—and she's so like her. Must she, too, learn her lesson by first breaking someone's heart?"

"Dear Jamy, let us hope and pray that she won't," said Heidi, putting her arm about her old school friend and speaking tenderly. "If you're fond of Max, don't give him up just because she has these tantrums. We'll work out something, with the dear Lord to help us."

Jamy sighed deeply. "Yes, surely with His help, it will not be as bad for Marta as it was for Grandmother. Her cross ought to help. It really ought."

They went inside then, for the air had grown quite cold and the babies had finished their nap and were demanding attention. Already Tobi reached for his spoon when Heidi tried to feed him his gruel. He would learn to help himself early.

Martali, however, made no effort to take the spoon, but only held her mouth open like a fledgling.

"Must you, too, depend on me?" said Heidi, holding the spoon away to see if she wouldn't attempt to take it herself. But Martali lay propped against her pillow, smiling sweetly and waiting to be fed.

"Dear Lord, make them strong!" Heidi suddenly prayed, leaning her head forward on the bare kitchen table and letting the spoon fall back in the bowl.

Brigitte came in and, seeing her thus, came forward and took the bowl and proceeded to feed Martali.

"You've tired yourself with all the young ones to look after," she scolded. "I see Marta's been screaming again and these twins alone are a handful. Why didn't you call me? I would have heard if you had shouted from the door."

"Where were you?" asked Heidi, for Brigitte looked weary herself. Her apron was turned halfway around towards the back and her hands were red as though she had done a washing.

"To the old weaver woman's," she answered. "Her daughter has come home with a sick husband and a baby that won't live through the night. Now there's another baby, a sickly little one, and Lisi so helpless——"

"I'll go over at once," said Heidi, her own trouble now appearing as nothing beside that of her neighbour. "I'll take them whatever they need. There are a few little shirts that Tobi and Martali have outgrown and there's some broth left from the meat Peter brought in. I think there's a little extra milk and some cakes——"

"May I help carry them?" asked Marta, appearing in the doorway. Her eyes were still swollen from crying, but the sleep had refreshed her and she stood there eager to help.

"Why, certainly," said Heidi, beginning to load her arms with the provisions. Perhaps this was the answer. Perhaps, through helping others, Marta would learn to help herself without first hurting someone as her grandmother had done before her.

Thankfully, Heidi now filled her own arms and she and the child walked through the gathering darkness to the humble hut of the old weaver woman. Brigitte watched them a moment, smiling, and when she returned to finish feeding the twins, Martali had the spoon in her hands and was patiently sucking what little gruel there was still clinging to the bowl.

Chapter 14

The Alm-Uncle's Secret

*I*t was a cold Autumn, and Winter set in early and promised to be a hard one. Now all the fir trees that had been green such a short while before wore great snowy plumes instead of branches and the ground sparkled and shone as though it were covered with millions of tiny jewels. Every day the cold grew more intense.

Heidi did not mind the cold for herself and her family as the manor house had such thick walls and had been so well restored that hardly a breath of the wintry air came through. But the hut of the weaver woman shook and rattled as if the strong winds might overturn it. By November it stood deep in snow, but this did not prevent Heidi from going every day with broth or fresh rolls or whatever was needed.

As long as it continued to fall, the deep snow was soft and Marta walked in Heidi's footsteps like a faithful shadow. But soon the sky cleared and a hard crust was over everything. Then Marta begged to be allowed to go alone and carry the supplies on her sled.

Tobi and Martali were growing so fast that there were many little garments to be given away. They learned as fast as they

grew, and when the coldest weather came they were able to
pull themselves up on their knees in order to be closer to the
blue and white tiles that made such a sheltered place for their
bed. They traced around the figures of animals and flowers that
were on the tiles and their eyes opened wider and they often
laughed and crowed. Marta shouted aloud at their pleasure
until, one day, she noticed that the thing which had pleased
them was not one of the flowered tiles or one of those with the
gay huntsmen or the laughing children. It was a hideous devil's
head on a goat's body. Martali touched it once more with her
tiny finger and then laughed and patted it with her whole
hand.

"Martali!" screamed Marta, pulling the little hand away. "It's
a bad picture. You mustn't touch it. It's the Evil One himself
and you mustn't go near him."

"Who told you of the Evil One?" asked Brigitte, turning to
her sharply.

"My schoolmates," Marta responded. "There's a picture in
one of my books and they say it's a bridge built by the devil. I
know the whole story. They built bridges and bridges and none
of them would hold together so, one night, the Bailiff was
returning home discouraged. He kept saying over and over to
himself. 'The Evil One himself couldn't build a bridge over the
wild Reuss and make it hold together.' Then, what do you
think? A voice spoke to him *and it was the Evil One.* 'So you
think I couldn't build a strong bridge?' he demanded. 'Well,
what will you give me to try it?' 'Anything,' said the Bailiff. He
didn't think what he was saying until the Evil One answered,
'Very well, the first living being that sets foot on the bridge
belongs to me.' "

"You are telling the story very well," said Brigitte when

Marta paused for breath. "But I know it already. It's only a legend and what can it prove?"

"Wait, and I will tell you," cried Marta, growing more excited. "You know that a goat was sent over the bridge to trick the Evil One and this made him so angry that he picked up a great rock and was about to throw it at the Bailiff when someone made the sign of the cross. Well, I was thinking that if Martali wore my cross then it wouldn't hurt her even if she did touch that picture. She'd be protected, just like the Bailiff was, and that's a true story too. I saw the Devil's Bridge once myself and the big stone is still there just where the Evil One dropped it. So there is an Evil Spirit, as well as a Good Spirit, and the Evil One watches Martali all the time because she didn't cry at the christening——"

"What nonsense is this?" Brigitte interrupted. "I never saw a child with such strange ideas in her head. Isn't there enough trouble in the world without anybody thinking up such foolishness as this?"

"But I didn't think it up," protested Marta, tears coming to her eyes. "I didn't——"

"Very well," interrupted Brigitte, anxious to avoid a tantrum. "Put your cross about Martali's neck if you think it will help, and then run out and play in the snow like other children."

"Oh, I will! I will!" cried Marta, so eager that she nearly fell over the bench in her haste to reach the crib. Martali now gave her full attention to the sparkling cross which Marta had hung about her neck and she no longer paid any attention to the pictures on the great tile stove.

A little later Jamy came into the living-room and, to her dismay, found the treasured cross with the ribbon all wet from being chewed. Martali was getting her first teeth and the cross to her was only something to bite on.

"Who has done such a thing?" cried Jamy. "Can Marta have no feeling for the dear grandmother who gave us this keepsake?"

Then Brigitte told her how it had happened and how she had avoided a tantrum by allowing Marta to place the cross about Martali's neck.

"And now," she finished, "she's out on her sled with the other children. It does my heart good to hear her laughing."

It was, indeed, a good thing for Marta to be playing outside once again with her schoolmates. The air, though cold, was sharp and exhilarating and Marta was warmly dressed in her hood and leggings. It was much better than seeing her constantly hovering over the babies' crib like a worried hen. But the cross! What was to be done about the cross?

"I suppose I might as well let Martali keep it," Jamy decided at last with a deep sigh. "Marta will feel better until she finds something new to fret about, and that won't be long—if I know my little sister."

But Marta's neck felt empty without the cross, now that she was used to wearing it, and soon she discovered that a string of beads or shells or any other trinket amused Martali and kept her hands away from the devil's picture on the tiles just as well as did the cross. Peter gave her a goat's bell to play with and this so charmed her that she dropped the cross on the floor and Marta would have stepped on it if she had not seen it just in time. Without a word, she placed it back on her neck and thought to herself how very pleased the grandma would be now that she was wearing it once more.

Marta had a way of entering a room noiselessly and hearing things that were meant for older ears. Still she had not learned to tell the truth from gossip and often, when Heidi sent her on errands to the bakery or to the dressmaker's little shop, she paused to listen to what the carpenter would have certainly called the sound of hammers driving crooked nails. Thus she heard it said that the Alm-Uncle was once possessed by the Devil and had to come down to the church in Dorfli to repent.

"No one knows who his wife was," Dame Barbel declared, nodding over the fresh rolls she had just purchased from the baker.

"Now that he's gone," the baker replied, "his secret is gone with him. But it was strange doings up there on the mountain alone like an eagle . . ."

He stopped then, seeing Marta holding her coin out for bread. But the child had heard and, true to Jamy's predictions, this gave her something new to fret about. When she reached home she went directly to Heidi and asked, "What was the Alm-Uncle's secret?"

The question came so suddenly and Heidi was so unprepared for it that for a moment she was unable to answer. Then, with a smile, she replied:

"A secret, Marta dear, is something nobody knows about. Once it is known, it ceases to be a secret. And so, you see, if my grandfather had a secret I would not have known it either. But he was a good man, whatever secrets he had."

"People shouldn't talk so then," said Marta as she handed Heidi the loaf of bread.

Jamy placed it on a board and stood, looking thoughtful, as she cut it into slices.

"What do you suppose Marta's been hearing?" she asked after the child had left the room.

"Probably only one of the gossips in the bakery still talking about my grandmother," Heidi replied. "They have never ceased to wonder who she was. I think Grandfather himself would have told me about her if he had lived a little longer. The day he died he mentioned her for the first time in his whole life and gave me a lock of her hair and the watch he's been keeping it in all these years."

"He must have loved her then," said Jamy thoughtfully.

"I've never doubted it. He was probably heart-broken when she died and so kept silent. He said he did not talk readily of things that were close to his heart. But why do you look at me so, Jamy? What are you thinking?"

"Nothing," she replied quietly, "except that possibly he kept silent because he did not wish to say anything unkind."

"But, Jamy, I don't understand at all——"

"Your grandfather was a soldier, wasn't he? You said he went to Naples to join the army. But I don't suppose you'd know when that was. Did Naples belong to France at the time? I've heard him mention an attempt to assassinate the Emperor of Austria. Was he in the Austrian army too, or don't you know?"

"I don't know," said Heidi. "But whatever war it was, and whatver army, his side was defeated. I'm sure of that. He's seen a lot of trouble. I wonder if you can be right and that his wife made it hard for him too."

"I'm pretty sure I'm right," said Jamy with a mysterious smile. "But first I shall write to Papa and find out all he knows about Grandmother. Her husband was an Austrian soldier too."

"Jamy, you don't mean . . ." Then Heidi stopped as the full import of what she was about to say dawned upon her. "But then they'd be the same! And we'd be cousins! Jamy! Jamy! Do you think it's really possible?"

"It might be. You say your grandfather never mentioned his

wife and that everybody blamed him for wasting his whole
fortune and not saying a word about where he went? Well, my
grandmother went through her husband's fortune and then left
him. And there were two boys! He took the older and she kept
the younger. But the thing that makes me feel this so strongly is
Marta's attachment for him. Wouldn't she, naturally, love her
own grandfather? And I've never forgotten the way he looked
at her when she said her name was Marta. The name probably
awoke all sorts of memories. And can you blame him for being
bitter after what happened?"

"And when he grew so angry about the coin . . . Oh, I see it
all now, but how can we know for sure?"

"We can't, unless Papa has some record of the family name.
Grandmother called herself Madame Kruse, but that was the
name of her parents, not her husband. Papa uses the name too
as it connects him with a distinguished Hungarian family.
Heidi, what was your grandfather's whole name?"

"Tobias Halm. It's in the church records. But nobody ever
called him anything but Uncle."

"Then little Tobi is named for him too?"

"Another Tobi and Martali," said Heidi, very low. "And he
suggested the names. If it's true, then he's forgiven her and
they're together now as they were on earth. Oh, it's all very
strange and it makes one feel there must be a golden thread
running through all our lives and a wonderful, wonderful plan."

"It reminds me of what Max says," mused Jamy. "He thinks
that even an earthquake or an avalanche has its purpose. He
says this beautiful country with its mountains and lakes and
numberless gorges never would have been as it is except for
rock-falls which must have been real catastrophes when they

happened. But that is forgotten now while the mountains are still as majestic as ever."

"What's all this talk of catastrophes?" asked Peter, coming in unexpectedly from his work of shovelling paths. "I just averted a minor catastrophe myself. Marta nearly ran me down with that swift new sled of hers."

Jamy and Heidi looked at each other and it was good to be able to laugh. But should they tell him? Heidi, deciding that since the grandfather had kept his secret this long, it would keep a little longer, looked up and said:

"That was a quotation from Max. Have you heard of Max Tauber, the eminent geologist? Jamy is thinking of annexing him to the family."

"What family?" asked Peter.

"Ours," said Heidi, squeezing Jamy's hand and hoping it was true.

Chapter 15

Tobi Makes a Discovery

*T*he answer that came from Jamy's father in Paris was disappointing in one respect, as he wrote that he knew as little about his family as Jamy did. In fact, he knew even less as he and his mother had never been close. She thought he gave too much time and thought to the business of making money and this had created a gulf between them. But, in another respect, the letter was most satisfactory. It was full of tender phrases such as Colonel Kruse had seldom put in any of his letters to either of his daughters and, furthermore, he stated that if these Swiss peasants really were his own kin he would certainly take some time off from his business and pay them a visit.

"Imagine my father coming here!" exclaimed Jamy, holding the letter against her heart.

"To get me?" asked Marta, her eyes becoming wide and frightened.

"Of course not, you timid little chamois, but just for a visit. Wouldn't you like to see him?"

"I don't know," said Marta quite truthfully.

"Well, it won't be for a while yet," Jamy reassured her. "The

117

weather is too cold and he is too busy. By Spring you may feel differently about it."

Marta's feelings, however, changed very little as the long Winter came to an end and the trees began to show their leaves.

Soon the first flowers were blooming and the goats were led out where they could eat the sweet, young grass once more and so give more milk for the children to drink. Peter's crops had done well the year before and he had saved nearly enough to buy a fine cow.

"How do you feel about it this year?" he asked his mother. "Is the climb up to the chalet on the Alm going to be too much for you?"

"It's pretty steep. I'm better at cooking than I am at mountain-climbing. I shall miss my large kitchen. But, Peterli," she begged, "do listen to me a moment. I have a plan."

And thereupon she told him how she had thought it all out. If she stayed in Dorfli and took in a few summer boarders there would be still more to spend on the farm.

"And if a mother can't help her own son," she finished as though the matter were settled once and for all, "I'd like to know who can."

"Very well, Mother," Peter agreed, "but if it becomes too hard for you, remember, Heidi is to come down and help. Have you any idea who your summer people will be?"

"Herr Sesemann and Clara will come. They always do. You'll be seeing plenty of them on the Alm as well, and if Chel comes home he would be sad indeed to see the doctor's house closed up and everybody gone. Besides," she stated matter-of-factly, "do you suppose I don't know it's better for a mother to look after her own children without the grandmother always interfering?"

"As if you ever interfered," Peter scolded gently.

"Very well," she retorted, "but I know what I know. You and Heidi will enjoy being alone with the children."

But it was agreed to wait until June, when school would be out and when Colonel Kruse would have made his visit to Jamy and Marta. The manor house would be far more suitable for entertaining an Austrian diplomat.

Marta trembled whenever the approaching visit was mentioned, as she felt positive her father was coming to take her away from Heidi. Then, when he wrote that his wife, Marie, was coming too, she was convinced of it. Several bad screaming spells interfered with her lessons and almost made her ill. But Jamy couldn't write and ask her parents not to come. She had grown genuinely fond of them during her Summer in Paris. Besides, Max was returning home for a visit at the same time and her father had taken a great liking to the interesting young scientist. Perhaps . . . but here Jamy would drift off into dreams that, in her more practical moments, seemed quite impossible because of the school and Marta's hysterics and the preoccupation of the young man himself in a book he was writing on the geology of Switzerland.

On the bright May morning that her mama and papa were expected Marta awoke with the feeling that her world was about to come to an end. The new green leaves of the young beech trees outside the garden wall sparkled and shimmered from a light rain that had fallen during the night. The apple trees were all in bloom and on the hedge the white thorn blossoms lay like new snow. The whole garden was sweet with the perfume that drifted up from the fragrant flower beds with

the ancient tiles, like fairy streets, between them. But Marta
saw nothing of all this. She sat on a bench, dressed in a
delicate print to receive her mama and papa, but with her head
down and great tears rolling down her cheeks. She would not
look at Tobi and Martali who kept tugging at her skirt and
begging her to play with them. They had passed their first
birthday and were both able to walk a little and to creep very
fast. Usually they crept because this took them where they
wanted to go a great deal faster than walking. Besides there
were all sorts of wonderful things a baby might discover while
creeping about in a garden. Some of these wonderful things
Tobi was able to call by name. But Martali said only one word.
To her, this word described everything she saw or felt or would
ever want to hold in her hand. It was *"Schön!"* pronounced
with a baby lisp.

"Schön! Schön!" she would call out whenever she discovered
a flower. The tiles that had once been the floor of the old hall
were *schön* to her, but to Tobi they were *stein.*

The twins had not played in the garden long before they
discovered that the tiles came loose and made splendid blocks.
It was while they were banging the tiles together and Martali
was shouting, "Schön!" and Tobi insisting, "Stein!" that Marta's mama and papa arrived in a coach.

Marta heard the clatter of horses' hoofs and the rumble of
wheels and knew they were there but, when all the others ran
out to greet them, she stayed in the garden trying to swallow
her tears.

"Well, where's Marta?" a voice boomed from inside the house.
"Let's see this strong, healthy girl who has fallen in love with
Switzerland. Marta! Marta!"

"She's in the garden. Marta!" called Heidi. "Your mama and

papa are here. Aren't you going to say 'how do you do' to them?"

Marta came in at last, her head down, her eyes red and swollen.

"What's this? Crying?" asked the papa. "They told me you were happy here."

"I am happy," said Marta, although her words were hardly audible through her sobs.

"She's afraid you've come to take her away," Jamy explained. "She has almost made herself ill worrying about it."

"A fine pair of parents we make," said the colonel with a pitying glance towards his wife. "Mother was right. We've made a god out of money and social position and destroyed what little love the children ever had for us. And now Marta is crying because she thinks we're going to take her home!"

"I have been a good mama to you, haven't I?" said Marie, taking a step towards the child. "I've given you everything——"

"No! No! No!" screamed Marta, stamping her foot. "I won't go back! I won't! I won't! I won't be left alone in the dark while you and Papa go out and leave me with horrid maids who slap me when I scream."

"They have to do something with you," Marie began helplessly.

"But not slap me! Heidi doesn't ever slap me and I don't have to scream and be afraid of things when I'm here because this house is safe. It's built on a rock. But in Paris everything rumbles and shakes at night and I wake up and scream. You don't want to hear me scream, do you? You don't want to hear me scream!"

"Can't you see you're upsetting your mother? Go on back to the garden," commanded the colonel harshly.

Marie turned to her older daughter in despair.

"Oh, Jamy," she reproached her. "You said she'd improve. But she's worse than ever. How can your friends stand it? How can they keep her here?"

"I don't know," Jamy replied with a hopeless gesture. "Heidi is an angel on earth or she would never do it."

"How can we thank you——" the colonel began, turning to Heidi.

"Don't thank me now," she begged. "Only wait until I have succeeded. Leave the child with me a little longer and I am sure you will see an improvement."

"We'll leave her with you until her schooling is done, if you will take her. We'll pay you well for her board and see that she has whatever clothes she needs. We are only too glad to have her off our hands," Colonel Kruse finished with a little groan.

"But, Maurice, you can't give up where your own child is concerned," his wife protested. "I've been selfish and let you do it before because her crying upset me. She knows that now. See how she takes advantage of it!"

"She never used to have those screaming spells when Mother was alive——"

"There you go again!" Marie exclaimed, raising her voice until it was easy to see how Marta might have inherited her mother's lack of self-control. "It's *mother*, this, and *mother* that! And from Marta all I used to hear was 'Grandma didn't do it so,' but the grandma isn't here to take care of her any more."

"That's the root of the whole trouble," the colonel explained. "My mother had complete charge of the children while she lived. But now it is up to us. Something must be done. Marta will be a young lady soon. She cannot go on like this. She must learn self-control, if nothing else. But where will she learn it?"

"I've tried to teach her," said Heidi, realizing the full extent of her failure. "But perhaps this summer it will be different. We're going up to the high pasture to live in the chalet. There will be room for Marta if you will allow us to take her. Up there something happens to you. No matter how ill or how unhappy you are, you suddenly find yourself glad to be alive. Of course, I cannot promise any miracles, but please let me try."

"Shall we?" asked the colonel, turning to his wife.

"And tell our friends that our little girl is staying with strangers? If Jamy comes home it will be as it was last year. Even Max thought it odd that we should have sent for Jamy and not Marta. Of course, if you could prove this relationship, it would make the explanations easier. But that isn't all. Jamy, what are those children screaming about in the garden?"

"It's the twins. They've found something again. Probably only a flower. They've been calling like that all day."

"Hear that baby lisp. To think that we left Marta with her grandmother and missed knowing her as a baby," the colonel reproached himself.

"Things might have been so different," sighed Marie, "if I had only been older and had known what I know now. Jamy and I were like sisters last summer. But Marta— Oh, what shall we do with Marta?"

"Schön! Schön! Stein! Stein!" called the twins louder and louder.

"They've really found something!" cried Marta, bursting into the room like a different child. "I wouldn't look at first, but then I did and it's another cross just like the one I'm wearing. Only this has something printed on it. *T.H. to M.K.* What do you suppose that means?"

"Excuse me for a moment," said Heidi, turning to her guests. Then she followed Marta back to the garden.

Tobi and Martali had torn up at least a dozen tiles. They were scattered far and wide and the two little faces were quite smudged. Heidi looked at her beautiful garden in dismay. Suppose the twins had decided to put one of the shining beetles into their mouths!

"But just see here!" Marta insisted. "It was tight in Tobi's hand. He must have found it under one of the tiles. You see, it is the other part of my cross. I know it is!"

And as she spoke, Marta fitted the hinges together and the plain cross became a locket just as it must have been when it was new.

"But what do the letters stand for?" Marta asked as Heidi kept looking at the cross with increasing wonder.

"*T.H.* to *M.K.*, Tobias Halm to Marta Kruse. Couldn't it be that, Marta?"

"Yes! Yes! Of course it could. But who was Tobias Halm?"

"That was my grandfather's name. Think hard," Heidi told her. "Do you remember when you opened his present and the paper was empty? Did you shake the paper so that anything could have fallen from it by accident? This cross is so small you could easily have dropped it."

"And it fell in the place where I had turned up the tile!" exclaimed Marta, now seeing very clearly what must have happened. "But where would the uncle find the other half of my cross?"

"He didn't find it, Marta darling. He had it all the time. Don't you see? Your grandmother's name was Marta Kruse, just like yours."

Still Marta could not comprehend.

"But she said my grandfather had the broken half of her cross. She said he kept it, meaning to fix it some time——"

"And now he has fixed it!" cried Heidi, kissing the flushed cheeks that had so recently been wet with tears. She held Marta very close for a moment; then stood her back to look at her. Yes, her hair was exactly the colour of that chestnut curl the grandfather had kept in his watch during all these years. Now Heidi was sure of it. The dear grandma Marta had been so fond of was her grandmother too. She and the grandfather had once been married and when they separated each of them kept half of the cross. Heidi's father had been brought up by the grandfather and Marta's father by the grandmother, but they were all one family, just as Jamy had hoped. But how strange that the cross should clear up all this after more than fifty years!

"But how has the grandfather fixed it?" asked Marta, still confused. "I don't see how the Alm-Uncle could have the cross if the grandfather fixed it. It was grandfather who kept the broken shell. He was always meaning to fix it——"

"Anyway," said Heidi, realising that it would take Marta a long while to understand anything as confusing as this, "he's fixed it so that you can go up on the Alm with us. Come, let's tell your mama and papa."

Chapter 16

A Promise
that was Kept

Marta stood in the centre of the garden clapping her hands and shouting, "We're going up on the Alm! We're going up on the Alm!"

There was no need for Heidi to call, or to go in and tell her parents. Everybody came running out when they heard her happy shouts.

The twins, imitating her, were shouting, "Alm! Alm!"

Now everybody was talking at once. Marta had no idea what they were saying or why Jamy and Heidi now called each other "cousin." Her mama and papa, who had been strangers a moment ago, were now Uncle Maurice and Aunt Marie and everybody was saying how wonderful it was that now it had all come right. Questions and answers flew back and forth so quickly that Marta did not even try to understand. After a while Heidi would explain it. Now it was enough to know that, somehow, the cross had worked this magic and granted her wish. It was enough to know that she would be allowed to stay with Heidi where everything was safe because of Heidi's faith.

The visit that had started off so badly now promised to be as joyous as a festival. Max was invited up from the parsonage

126

for luncheon and he and Peter carried the long table out under an apple tree which leaned over the garden wall and was fragrant with pink and white blossoms. One of the benches on which the family was to sit was placed against the ivy-covered wall while the other stood firmly on the tiles which were now back in their original places. Max had just finished putting down his end of the second bench when Marta surprised him by rushing forward and shaking his hand.

"How do you do, Cousin Max," she said.

"Well, now that's what I call a hearty greeting," he responded with a pleased expression on his face. "But how do you explain the relationship?"

"Oh, we're all cousins and uncles and aunts now," Marta told him happily, "and I belong to this family. I really belong!"

"What is all this?" asked the bewildered young man, turning to Jamy. "Does this mean that I belong too? It's really not a bad idea."

"Oh, Max! We've hardly said 'how do you do' to each other."

"Well, there must be some reason for this celebration. But hasn't your little sister mixed things up somewhat? It should be Brother Max. The bride's little sister usually speaks of the groom as 'brother.' "

"You shouldn't say such things right before all these people," Jamy protested, blushing furiously.

"Then let's walk outside under the apple trees and I'll say them to you alone."

The colonel and his wife watched the young couple from where they were standing beside the rose trellis. She shivered a little and he put his arm around her.

"It looks as though we've lost both our daughters."

"We never had them," said Marie sadly. "I thought good

times were all that mattered and you thought it was your duty
to entertain all the visiting officers and Marta frightened me
with her tears and Jamy was never happy with us until last
Summer when she met Max. I suppose we deserve this," she
finished, "but do you remember how we kept telling each other
we were doing everything for them?"

"Fooling ourselves," the colonel answered. "Well there's no
use doing that any longer. Jamy is happier with Max, and
Marta with Heidi. Now we can go back to our entertaining and
try and forget what a mess we've made of bringing up our
children."

Marta, seeing her parents standing thus, ran over to them
and squeezed in between them.

"Aren't you glad I'm going to stay?" she asked brightly. "I
won't be any trouble to you now and you won't ever have to
hear me scream. I thought you wanted me out of the way, but
you don't look very happy about it."

"We'll miss not having any daughters," her papa said. "Jamy
and Max will be getting married——"

"But that won't make any difference, will it?" Marta asked,
suddenly anxious.

"Any difference? But of course it will make a difference.
Jamy will not come home to us after she's married to Max and
you will be here——"

"Oh," said Marta, relieved. "I meant any difference about
my staying here. I don't mind Jamy's getting married if I can
still stay with Heidi. But who will teach the school?"

"Some new teacher," the colonel replied a little impatiently.

"But I can still go, can't I? I can keep on going to school in
Dorfli?"

"I suppose so, as long as you stay——"

"But you said I might stay. You said I might go up to the chalet on the Alm with Heidi and Peter. You said——"

"Yes, yes, my dear," Marie interrupted, anxious to avert a tantrum, "we did say you might. But you must say 'Cousin Heidi' and 'Cousin Peter.' It sounds better for a child to address her elders so."

"Then may I stay with Cousin Heidi?"

The colonel and his wife looked at each other. For a minute their eyes met in a long, understanding glance. Then he spoke slowly:

"After all, these people are my own kin, and if Marta is happier living with them, I don't see why we should force her to come with us. She doesn't like Paris and she never cared for the château in Vaud after her grandmother died there. We may as well admit it, she does look healthier. I suppose she is better off here."

"Of course she is," agreed Marie, patting Marta's curls as she spoke. "Now don't you worry about your mama and papa. They'll be having good times in Paris just as they've always had, and in the summer there will be the big château in Vaud with so many, many rooms for guests and parties. Everything will be all right, Marta. We won't take you away. We won't ever take you with us until you really want to come."

"You're good to me. I wish I hadn't screamed at you," said Marta, afraid that her screaming had caused them to look so sad. Then she hugged her papa and kissed her mama quickly on the cheek. "Now I'm going to help Cousin Heidi set the table under the trees for our party. You'll see I won't be any trouble to her." And she ran off, never noticing that her mama had borrowed her papa's large handkerchief to wipe away her tears.

A little later Marta was allowed to ring the bell that called the reunited family to table.

The long table under the apple tree was charmingly set with many tempting foods. Marta glanced at her mama and papa from time to time, afraid that she might have put their forks in the wrong place or their knives on the left instead of the right. The table at home had been set with such care that she was never allowed to touch it. But here things were done so simply and easily that anyone could help. Even Tobi and Martali were allowed to carry their own pewter milk mugs to the table and, small as they were, they understood that they must be quiet a moment before they began eating and say "thank you" for the food.

This time Colonel Kruse felt it was his duty to thank the Lord for finding his father, even though it was too late for him ever to meet him and even though it did mean turning over his daughter to the cousins she loved better than her own parents. Such a prayer took quite a while to compose and, if the Lord understood it, He did a great deal better than Marta. To her the words only made the relationship all the more confusing. His father? Was the Alm-Uncle really her papa's father? Then how could they be so different? Only one thing was clear from the lengthy prayer. Her papa was thankful that she was going to stay with Heidi. She looked up, trying to say a little "thank you" of her own.

Overhead the apple blossoms were like a pink ceiling and Marta, looking up at them, thought at first that each blossom had a friendly face. But then she saw through them to the sky beyond, where every moment flying clouds scudded across the sun. A fear rose in her heart that suddenly she might find the apple blossoms gone and that reaching hand in the clouds

again. The hand that would snatch her away from Heidi just
when she was beginning to find the peace and contentment
that she had lost in the death of first the grandmother and then
the Alm-Uncle whom she was supposed to call "grandfather"
now. But why that was, or how any of it had happened, she
had failed to comprehend.

Since the visit of her parents was not to bring the separation
she feared, the time passed pleasantly for Marta. The house was
in a state of continual excitement and every meal was a festive
occasion. In the kitchen there was always some kneading and
baking under way.

"Come, try these," Brigitte would call out as soon as Marta's
face appeared in the doorway.

Then a golden yellow apple cake or a round plum tart would
be already on a plate for her.

"Are these good enough for your mama and papa? Yes, yes,
let Martali have a taste. Here are some raisins for Tobi."

Then the children would run out to the garden where the
family usually ate on clear days and there Heidi would be
arranging the dessert.

"Let me help," Marta always begged. And when some of the
single raisins would fall from the bunches of blue dried grapes
beside the plate and some of the almonds piled on top would
roll down, Marta was alowed to fill the pockets of her pinafore
for an afternoon treat.

The colonel and his wife walked about a great deal by
themselves and could not say enough in praise of the glorious
mountain scenery.

"Marta belongs here," they would tell each other. And she
would smile at them happily, confident now that nothing would
change their minds. Thus the week flew by, and at last the

whole family was gathered around the packed travelling carriage
and the visitors were ready to leave. Max, at the last moment,
led Jamy's father aside and asked him if it would please him to
have a large wedding at the château in Vaud.

Then Marta, who had overheard what had been said, asked
anxiously, "And will I have to come?"

"Won't you want to, child?"

"No," she declared, "I won't. And, Papa, don't forget that
you thanked God that I would be happy and said you'd never
take me away until I really wanted to come."

"I'll keep that promise," the colonel declared with feeling.
"But some day you will come. You belong to a courageous
family, Marta, and God won't let you stay away forever."

"Won't He?" asked Marta, turning her face towards the sky.
Then the hand was still there. Everything was not all right, as
she had supposed. She glanced towards her mama and found
her wiping away tears. What could it mean? Didn't they want to
have good times and have her out of the way? Could she have
been mistaken? But then the memory of the conversation she
had overheard from behind a door flashed before her mind like
a picture. Her papa walking back and forth like an animal in a
cage, and saying over and over again:

"We'll have to put her in a school somewhere. Anything to
get her off our hands. How can we hope to entertain our friends
with a child who raises the roof of the house whenever she
doesn't have her way?"

And her mama, as always, blaming the kind grandma because, as she put it, "She spoiled the children with too much
love."

And so it had gone on—the same quarrel over and over. But

when she was not there she felt sure her parents never quar-
relled. They were always so gracious before their guests.

"Yes," thought Marta, "even if they do want me a little now,
it's better for me not to go."

Thus it came about that when Peter and Heidi moved up to
the Alm with all their belongings, Marta joined the procession
and walked proudly beside Dame, the new cow. Around the
cow's neck was a huge wreath of flowers which Marta had
woven and which Martali's tiny hands had helped fix in its
place. The cowbells jangled as the procession moved along,
followed by wagons on which were piled pots, cauldrons, presses
and everything that would be needed for cheese-making.

Little Tobi rode on his father's back while Peter's voice led
all the others in singing:

> "Come! Come! One and all,
> The lean, the fat,
> The large, the small,
> Up to the pastures come!
> Ha! Ha! Lioba!"

It was the first time Marta had heard the words to the song
that would, for the rest of her life, send a wave of homesickness
over her whenever it was played away from the Alm.

Chapter 17

Up on the Alm

*T*hree years had passed and again warm June had come with all its wealth of blue and yellow and crimson flowers and its fields of glowing berries. Marta, for the third time, had come up to the chalet on the Alm, with Peter and Heidi and the twins. Brigitte, as usual, was happy in the village keeping house for her summer people. Colonel Kruse and his wife had been counted among them as each summer they had come to visit Marta, even though she had not felt it necessary to go to them or to attend her sister's wedding at the château in Vaud.

Tobi was now a sturdy little boy of four and everything his father did was interesting and wonderful to him. Often he followed Peter about his work of cheese-making while Martali, as sturdy and rosy-cheeked as Tobi, ran beside him or, tiring of this, begged Marta to take her to the pasture. Then Tobi, not to be left out, would run behind them cracking his little whip.

"To the pasture! To the pasture!" all three children would shout, following the sound of clanging cowbells until they had reached the sunny pasture. From the slopes above could be heard the tinkling of the smaller bells worn by the goats, and together, they made a peaceful sound which carried to the village far below and delighted the heart of everyone who heard it.

Peter now owned six of the finest cows to be had in all the Prattigau valley and was chief herder for the cows from Maienfeld which were pastured on the Alm during the summer. He was known as Chief to his helpers and was as much the master of his little world as the skipper on the bridge of a ship. Full responsibility for the cows, the men and the cheese-making were in his hands. He employed two regular helpers in his cheese factory which, according to the grandfather's wish, he had established in the building intended for a shop. The shelves were now lined with enormous cheeses, each weighing more than eighty pounds and looking like large yellow wheels.

Peter had to see to it that the cheeses were regularly washed and salted until the eyes were large enough. Then he knew he had good Swiss cheese which would bring a fair price in the market.

Tobi and Martali really thought they were old enough to help him. But usually they could do little besides watch as he poured the milk into the kettle where it would turn into cheese. They were not strong enough to help stir it after it began to curdle. But Marta was. Often Peter told her she was as much help as a boy.

Where she helped most was in the pasture watching the cattle. This was not work, as cheese-making was, for the cows were gentle animals and seldom strayed beyond their pasture. Thoni still tended the goats on the slopes above as they liked tough herbs that the cows could not eat. Now he and Marta were good friends and when she was not needed to watch the cows she often climbed to the higher pastures with him. At such times Martali would follow, calling: "Martali go too! Martali go too!" in such a pleading chant that Marta could seldom resist her.

Tobi never called and pleaded as his sister did, but simply trotted along behind her.

"I took care of Martali," was his usual excuse, although Martali seemed well able to take care of herself.

Heidi, who loved the Alm just as dearly as she had ever loved it, kept herself busy in and about the chalet where she could hear the wind in the larch trees singing or sobbing, depending on her mood. Often she took up her violin in the evening while Peter's helpers joined the family in singing or dancing to the music. Already Martali had a clear, sweet voice and Marta could put such spirit into the herdsman's favourite song that anyone might think she had lived her whole life among the cattle.

On still evenings the Alm would echo with the haunting strains of music and the larch trees, with the wind singing and sighing through their branches, would join the chorus:

> *"Come! Come! Large and small,*
> *The old, the young,*
> *The short, the tall——*
> *Under the larch trees come!*
> *Ha! Ha! Lioba!"*

This evening the strains of music were especially sad and the great trees sobbed more often than they sang for Marta. Soon these beautiful days and enchanting song-filled evenings would be at an end. She had completed her schooling in Dorfli under the expert teaching of the young schoolmaster who had succeeded Jamy, and the following letter from her mama left no question at all in Marta's mind as to what was expected of her:

Chère Marta:

This summer your papa and I are not coming to visit you in Dorfli in the hope that you will come to us instead. Now your school days are over and you and I are both older and wiser . . . (Her mama had looked older, Marta thought, the last time she came to visit) *. . . I believe we could get along. Won't you give us another chance? We are very lonely and would love to have you with us here at the château for at least a month before school opens in the autumn.*

If we have made mistakes, as I know we have, won't you forgive us and grant this one request? Heidi has Tobi and Martali, but we have no one. We still entertain, but to what purpose? We would gladly give up every friend we have for the sake of having you with us again. Sometimes we fear we have lost you completely. But remember, we are not saying that you must come to the château. Come only if you really want to—only if you love us.

Max and Jamy expect to be with us for a little while, but Max can never stay in one place for very long because of his work. Jamy has suggested that you attend the school at Rosiaz where she and Heidi met. If you went there you could come home every week-end and be with us at the château as it is only two hours from Lausanne . . .

Marta read the letter this far and put it down. It had been in the old château in Vaud that her grandma had died.

She still remembered how the halls had thrown back a ghostly echo every time she screamed. This had only caused her to scream all the louder and the thought of going back there

terrified her more than the idea of a strange school where all
the students would stare at her and ask questions.

She finished reading the letter, which contained little else
except a tender "au revoir," and then gave it to Heidi who read
it and laid it aside without a word.

That night Marta went quietly to her room in the loft of the
little chalet. She lay down on her bed and although it was high
and fragrant as the tick had just been filled with new hay, she
could not sleep. The stars shone in through her window as
much as to say, "You will not be as near us in Vaud as you are
on the Alm."

The larch trees sobbed and sobbed. Marta could almost hear
their voices, "You will not have us to sing you to sleep in
Vaud."

For it was in Canton Vaud, beside the lake, that both the
school and the château were located.

Marta tried to remember the lake as something beautiful to
which she could look forward. But the wet mist which continually hung over it blurred the picture. It was all too sad to
contemplate and at last she fell into a restless sleep.

The beaming sun, sending rays of gold into her window,
awoke her the following morning. She dressed quickly and
came down to find the family already at breakfast out under the
larch trees.

"It is a good thing you are here," Peter greeted her, "for Tobi
and Martali intend to help me with my cheese-making while
you and Heidi go for a walk. She tells me she's never taken you
to our enchanted garden."

"Is it far?" asked Marta, turning to Heidi without enthusiasm.

"It won't seem far," she answered, "as I have so much to talk
over with you on the way."

"Now it is coming," thought Marta to herself, for she knew very well what was right and what Heidi would expect her to do. This knowledge lay like a heavy stone upon her heart. The twins' happy chatter did not call forth her usual smiles and cheerful retorts and her large golden pieces of toasted cheese remained untouched on her plate.

"Come, eat a little breakfast," Heidi urged her. "It is a long walk and we are only taking a light lunch along with us. We won't need to carry anything to drink as there will be strawberries to eat when we are thirsty."

"Strawberries! Strawberries!" cried Martali, running to fetch the baskets. "May I pick some too?"

"It is too far for your little legs to travel," Heidi replied, "but we will bring home full baskets and you may have some for supper."

"I'm strong," announced Tobi, showing his muscles. "I can travel."

"But not today," Heidi told him. "Marta and I want to talk; besides, your papa needs you to help him scour the big kettle. Today it must shine so that you can see your face inside."

"I'll shine it," Tobi promised, rubbing his fist on the table to show how well he would do it.

"But I don't want to shine the big kettle," Martali protested.

"Then you shall stand up on the high stool and hang out the cheese strainers for me——"

"But I don't want to. I want to pick strawberries with Mama and Marta——"

"I'm afraid they are going to be difficult, Peter," said Heidi, beginning to feel a little anxious about leaving them.

"I'll look after them," he promised. "Come, children, send

the travellers off with a song." And he began beating time with a spoon while the twins followed him in singing:

> *"Good luck be yours,*
> *Rich cheese and bread,*
> *Into the cheese room come!*
> *Ha! Ha! Lioba!"*

The music was almost too much for Marta. Her heart beat so loudly she was almost afraid Heidi could hear it as the two of them started up the grassy slope. They climbed for a while in silence then Heidi said:

"You must wonder why we're taking this unexpected holiday. Well, I shall tell you. There is a story I want you to hear and since it has a very beautiful lesson for you, I want you to be in the loveliest garden in all the world while I tell it."

"Is it another Bible story like the one about the wind?" asked Marta.

"No, not this time. It's the story of a little girl like yourself who wanted to be happy."

"Oh," said Marta, relieved, "I thought you were going to tell me——"

"What?" asked Heidi, as she paused without finishing her sentence.

"That I must do as Mama says in the letter. I thought surely you were going to tell me that, and now I find it is only a story. Aren't you going to talk about the letter at all? Aren't you going to advise me at all? What shall I tell her in my answer?"

"That is for you to decide," Heidi replied. "After you have heard this story I shall leave you to make your own decision. I think, by then, you will know what is best."

"But to go away from all this!" And Marta threw out her arms as if to include the whole of the flower-studded field through which they had just passed, as well as the green forested cliffs that rose sheer above them. Fiery red alpine roses glowed between moss-covered stones and here and there isolated larches showed patches of deep blue sky through their swaying branches. Farther on the trees grew closer together and here and there fallen trunks and dead branches lay on the ground. Here Heidi cleared the path by pushing aside whatever branches were in the way and holding out her hand to help Marta over the rocks.

The sun was shining from a cloudless sky, growing constantly brighter as they climbed. The high snow mountains stood out completely behind the wooded heights and the twin summits shimmered faintly in the sunlight. But gradually the fir trees thinned and now they had come to a meadow near the top. As they entered the wide space thousands of little bells and stars nodded at them from their slender stems.

"Come! Come!" they seemed to call and beckon while the gentle breeze playing through them made a faint, dreamy tune.

Marta ran ahead, entranced by all the glowing flowers. Here and there a bright butterfly danced among them. Birds piped to each other and all around sounded the soft humming of a chorus of little insects.

"Oh, Heidi! Heidi!" Marta exclaimed at last. "This is your garden. I know it even though you have not told me. Do you suppose in Heaven it is any more beautiful than this?"

"I sometimes think that Heaven is all around us, if we only have eyes to see it," Heidi said softly.

"And on the Alm too?" questioned Marta.

"Yes, and in Dorfli. Even in the château which seems so

gloomy now. There must be a little Heaven there as well. And if not, Marta, why not make it so?"

"I could make Mama happier—and Papa too. But they never did very much to make me happy, so why should I?"

"You don't understand that, do you, Marta? That's why I brought you here. Up here you will feel closer to the things you don't understand and that may help you to decide what is best. Now shall we sit here while I tell my story?"

And Heidi motioned her to a little moss-covered mound where they might sit together among the flowers, but without crushing a single open cup.

Chapter 18

In the Enchanted Garden

"Is it a sad story?" asked Marta, leaning her head against Heidi's shoulder, prepared to listen. "Does it begin with 'Once upon a time'?"

"Listen and you shall soon hear," Heidi told her. "Once upon a time there lived a young girl with blue eyes and chestnut hair——"

"Just like mine?" interrupted Marta.

"Yes, dear. Exactly like yours. She was born in Austria and lived there with two loving parents who gave her everything she wanted. There was a war going on at the time and, as her papa worked in a large factory where they made guns and ammunition, he became very rich. At first this was all the little girl knew of the war. There was talk about a French alliance with Sardinia, about a loan to the enemy of five hundred million francs, and there were reports of battle after battle in which the Austrians were defeated. Still, her papa was making money and so she couldn't understand that the government no longer had enough to pay its soldiers and that for a long time they had received no money at all.

"The troops often marched through the town where she lived

143

and to her the soldiers looked very splendid in their uniforms. She used to watch them marching and thrill to the music just as you do when you hear the herdsman's song. Girls married very early in those days and so it did not take our little girl very long to fall in love with one of these soldiers—a brave young Swiss who had joined up to fight for Austria. One evening, when the band was playing and all the soldiers were marching, these two stole away to a church and were secretly married. Now, of course, you understand that such a secret could not be kept very long, and when the girl's father found out about it, he was extremely angry.

" 'Go with this soldier if you will,' he told her, 'but if you ever wish to return to your father's house you must come without him.'

"It was a stern command. But the girl was very much in love with her handsome soldier and made her choice. But, as I told you, she did not realise that the Austrians had no money left to pay their soldiers for fighting. She did not realise that this young soldier was fighting for Austria, not for money, but only because he loved the girl and her country. Such a thing did not seem possible to this girl who had always had maids and fine clothes and rich jewels just for the asking.

"For a while the soldier tried to give her these things to which she had been accustomed, but soon he had spent all his money and had to write home to his parents in Switzerland and beg them to help him. Still the girl was not satisfied. She had a beautiful home and a loving husband and two very dear children. But that was not enough. The war was over now. Austria had lost but the girl's father had purchased a beautiful château on Lake Geneva and moved to Switzerland. He still had just as much money as ever and, that being the case, she simply couldn't understand how her husband could be poor. He worked very hard, but nothing that he did was enough. Whenever the girl would see something in the shops that she wanted, she would beg and cry for it until he would buy it.

"One day she saw a beautiful cross in a shop window. There were diamonds in it, and diamonds, as you know, cost a great deal. Nothing would do but that she must have it.

" 'Very well,' said her husband. 'If you buy that cross, you shall wear it. For it will take my last sou.'

"The cross was bought and the very next week her husband received the sad news that his parents had died and their farm had been sold to pay their debts. This was too much for him. He seized the cross and tore it in half, saying, 'Now we shall share the cross. From now on we shall both carry a part of the burden.'

"Now their money was gone and it was necessary for them to move into a very poor hut where the wife herself must wash the children's clothes and cook the meals with hardly enough money coming in to buy a crust of bread. The husband's work paid him very little. The war had left Austria crushed and beaten. The older son tried to help his father, but the wife did not try. She only fretted and sobbed because her marriage had brought her so much less than she had when she was a little girl. At last the husband grew tired of all this fretting.

" 'Very well,' he said, 'if your parents can do so much more for you than I can, go to them. At least the children will have clean clothes and enough bread to keep them from starving!'

"The wife went, taking the baby. But the older son stayed with his father because he had learned to work and wanted to help him. Now the wife had all the money she wanted to spend. She had a maid. She had fine clothes again. She had a

nurse for her baby and they lived in luxury in her parents' large
château. Still she was not happy. She realised all she had lost
and longed to see her husband and other son again. But when
she wrote, begging them to forgive her, the letters were
unanswered.

"You see, the husband had gone back to his native place
with his older son and here every door had been shut against
them. Everybody he met blamed him for treating his parents so
badly. They said it was because of him that they had died in
poverty. And, because it was his wife's fault and he was too
loyal to say anything against her, he could not explain it. But
he grew more and more bitter against her. At last he moved to
another hamlet where he brought up his son and taught him to
work with a hammer and nails. Together they repaired an old
house and moved into it. The son became a fine carpenter, and
later, he brought home a lovely young wife. These two were
very happy for a time and the father was very proud of his son.
But one day, while working on a house, a beam fell on the son
and he was killed. His wife could not stand the shock and in
two weeks she followed him to the grave. But, instead of feeling
sorry for the poor father, the neighbours all blamed him, saying
the Lord had punished him for treating his own parents so
badly. Still he never spoke a word against his wife. He kept his
life story a secret and moved into a hut on a high cliff where he
would be alone with his trouble. Beyond this hut was a beautiful slope which was once used as a pasture. Thus the whole
slope was called the Alm, meaning 'the pastureland.' And,
because the villagers were distantly related to him, they called
the man who lived there 'the Alm-Uncle.' "

"Then this is a true story you're telling!" exclaimed Marta,
sitting up in surprise. Up until now she had been leaning

against Heidi's shoulder and listening to the story as though it were a fairy tale.

"What do you think it is?" Heidi asked. "Doesn't it sound as though it might have happened?"

"Part of it does. But if it is true, then this girl is my grandma and I can't believe my dear grandma was ever as unkind as you say she was in the story. I know she was married to the grandfather. I know they separated and each of them took a child. And the cross in the story was my cross. But Grandma couldn't have been as unkind as that. You didn't know her, or you would never think such a thing."

"I feel that I knew her, Marta darling, through her prayer. And I have not made up this story. Your grandmother told it to Jamy and what she didn't tell, I knew from my grandfather's life. I think, in her heart, your grandma was always kind. But she was afraid to do what she knew was right. When she had learned her lesson, my grandfather was not ready to forgive her. Perhaps you understand now why he looked at you as he did when he first heard that your name was Marta. You reminded him of his wife, and then, when you were so kind to him, it was almost as if your grandmother were there doing all the tender things she had failed to do during her lifetime."

"But she did them for me. She did everything possible for me. She was the best grandma in all the world."

"Yes, yes, dear Marta, I believe it," said Heidi. "She knew how it felt to do wrong and not be forgiven. All her life she tried to make up for the wrong she had done her husband. That was her cross. Now it belongs to you. It says, 'Have courage' and it also says, 'Be ready to forgive!' Now do you see why I have told you this story?"

" 'Have courage!' 'Be ready to forgive!' " Marta repeated,

touching the cross she wore about her neck. The half her grandmother had kept said, "Have courage" and the half that had belonged to the Alm-Uncle said, "Be ready to forgive."

"You see, Marta," Heidi spoke softly, "we may learn through the mistakes of others. We don't always need to wait until we have hurt someone dear to us. Now shall we continue our walk?"

"Yes, indeed!" cried Marta, jumping up and running on ahead. "I feel quite rested now, and I want you to show me all of this beautiful garden."

Flowers seemed to stretch ahead to the very sky and it was hard to tell where the blue harebells ended and the blue sky began. The garden sloped upward and the flowers grew even larger and brighter as they climbed.

Marta was running up the slope like a young deer, but suddenly she stopped as a miracle seemed to take place before her eyes. A broad stream, gleaming like silver, spread right across the field of glowing flowers. But everything was still. It made not the slightest sound or motion.

"Am I dreaming?" asked Marta, turning to Heidi with wide-open eyes. "How can a stream of water be so silent?"

Then Heidi told her that it was not a stream of running water that she saw, but a glorious broad glacier. It snaked down the steep, rocky gorge until it came to life and became a waterfall in the valley. But here it was a stream of silver ice.

"A glacier!" breathed Marta, her eyes fastened upon it. "But, Heidi, it's beautiful."

"Indeed it is," agreed Heidi. "Did you think it would be anything else?"

"Germaine said . . . Germaine said . . ." Marta stammered. But she couldn't say another word. The glacier held her, as

though in a spell; she looked and looked. She clasped and
unclasped her hands and, as she watched, a strange blue fire
flashed before her eyes.

She turned away, after a long moment, still speechless. It
seemed to her that at last she had seen such splendour that,
wherever she went, it would stay before her eyes. No matter
what happened, she had lived through this moment. Even if
she should go to the dismal old château there would still be
something—something to which she could turn when she needed
courage. She closed her eyes to see if the darkness shut it out.

"You'll stumble, walking along with your eyes shut," laughed
Heidi. "Is all this splendour too much for you to look at?"

"I'm trying to imagine what it will be like when I can't see it
any more," Marta answered.

"And is it as dark as all that?"

"But it isn't dark!" exclaimed Marta. "It's still there. The
lovely blue light and everything. I shall always see it. Always
and always."

"And have you never seen that Light before, dearest Marta?"

"No, never," she replied. "I used to see a hand in the sky
and it seemed as if it was always reaching. I thought it was
God. And, Heidi, I still don't see how if He's up there in the
sky, He can watch over so many of us down here. He would
have to have a great many eyes, like a giant——" She shud-
dered. "No! No! I'd rather not think of God at all. I'd rather
think of this."

"But maybe this is God. 'I am the Light!' 'I am the Truth!'
'God is Love!' We are told all this. But we have never been told
that He is a reaching hand. And in that very beautiful prayer
that the good grandma taught you, it says, 'Dear Spirit, dwell in

me.' So, if He is in your heart, Marta, how can He be a hand to reach down out of the sky?"

"I suppose He can't be," Marta agreed with a great sigh. She was silent a moment and then she said: "Heidi, would it be very silly to sing that prayer now, before we look for strawberries? I think now I can understand it."

Together their voices rose and because there was no one but God and His tiny creatures to hear it, the hymn became still sweeter, mixed with the trill of the birds and the lazy hum of countless insects who hovered over the flowers, their wings shimmering like petals in the sun.

> *"I need a kinder heart;*
> *Dear Spirit, dwell in me,*
> *Help me to live and love and work*
> *And of more service be.*
>
> *"I need a stronger will;*
> *Eternal One Divine,*
> *Oh, strengthen me and make my thoughts*
> *In harmony with Thine."*

Now, at last, it seemed to Marta that her thoughts were in harmony. No doubts, no fears, nothing but peace and harmony filled her heart as she joined hands with Heidi and went on singing:

> *"I need a broader mind;*
> *Dear Spirit, make me see*
> *That all who struggle here in pain*
> *Are labouring for Thee."*

And when they came to the last verse:

> *"I need a purer life;*
> *Dear Spirit from above,*
> *Drop Thy still dews of faith and peace*
> *And Thy eternal love."*

Marta held out her hand, as if she could feel it. Then she caught a glimpse of something that looked like strawberries. Could that be the glowing red field which stretched a short distance down the slope? Eagerly she ran along as if she had wings, only stopping when Heidi warned her of the deep gorge just beyond the slope she was descending.

"But if you look out across it you will see the whole valley and mountains beyond it."

"And the waterfall!" cried Marta, standing almost at the edge of the precipice. "Look! Look! From here I can see where the glacier changes into a waterfall."

Below, everything shimmered and glowed and the snow-white foam from the waterfall sent forth dazzling flashes of colour. Above, a shining stream of ice extended down into the valley, and at her feet were such large juicy berries that Marta felt sure they must taste more delicious than any others. She began picking, pausing every now and then to exclaim:

"Do you think I can explain it a little bit to Martali? Do you think she will understand how beautiful it was where they grew? Heidi, how long will it be before the twins can come here? Will you take them sometime when they're troubled about something and need help as I did?"

Finally, when her basket was almost filled, she stopped picking altogether and exclaimed: "Strawberries on the edge of a glacier! And it's even more wonderful than I expected. Everything is much much, much more wonderful!"

Chapter 19

At the End of the Day

*H*eidi and Marta were ready to return home. Their baskets were full of strawberries and their hearts were full to overflowing with thankfulness for a day neither of them would ever forget.

It was still early when they left the enchanted garden and started down the more difficult path through a rocky gorge. They were just approaching a steep, forested hillside when a shout rang out through the trees. Then Peter appeared with little Tobi riding on his shoulders. Heidi knew immediately that something was wrong.

"Why are you here?" she gasped. "Where's Martali?"

"She said she wanted to go with Mama," Tobi announced, looking down importantly from his high perch.

"Yes, Heidi," Peter said grimly. "She called after you for several hours after you left and, when I wasn't looking, she ran out into the fields. We've been searching for her ever since, Tobi and I. My helpers are looking too but, so far, we have found no trace of her. I thought surely she would be with you——"

His disappointment and grief showed clearly on his face.

Marta looked up at him, trying to make herself realise that this
had come at the end of her beautiful day.

"No, no, Peter. It can't be," she cried out suddenly. "She's
safe, wherever she is. She can't be really lost. Such a thing
couldn't happen. It couldn't!" She grasped her cross, holding it
very tightly in her hands.

"That's right," said Heidi, placing her hand firmly over
Marta's. "It says 'Have courage' and both of us need it now.
But, Peter, suppose she has come home while you were search-
ing. Is anybody there?"

"No. Nobody at all. We are all out looking for the child."

"But someone must be there. She mustn't come home to an
empty house. I will hurry ahead at once and blow the Alp horn
if she is found."

"Here," said Marta, thrusting her strawberry basket in Heidi's
hand. "Take these. She will like them. I think I'll stay here and
help Peter hunt."

"You might as well go with Heidi. You will be of no use——"
Peter began, but Marta's flashing eyes stopped him.

"I'll go this way," she announced, and darted off, following a
break in the undergrowth which Martali might have mistaken
for a path.

A little farther along she stopped and shouted:

"Martali! Martali! Martali!"

"Tali! Tali! Tali!" came back from the grey rocks in answer
to her shout.

It had been a long time since Marta had heard her own echo
answer her so plainly. It reminded her of the echoes that used
to live in the old château and scream back so frightfully whenever she had one of her crying spells.

"Martali! Martali! Martali!" she called again, determined not to let the echo frighten her.

Now it answered back like a voice, comforting her as she went deeper and deeper into the tangled underbrush. A little brown marmot rose up on his haunches just ahead of her, looked at her a moment, and then scurried into his hole.

"He's afraid," thought Marta, "but I'm not. Poor little Martali is probably afraid too, wherever she is. I must find her."

She ran on and on. She no longer knew in what direction she was going, but now the trees grew more thickly and a faint sound could be heard through the wavering branches. At first it sounded like a child's sobbing but as she came nearer Marta recognised it as the sound of a bubbling mountain brook. She must be far below the glacier, perhaps near the waterfall. But no, the gorge was so steep she could never get down there. This was some other brook. She followed the sound and it grew constantly louder until her calling could hardly be heard above the roaring and thundering of the water. Then she saw it, hurling itself down a steep ravine and leaping up again with a frightful roar whenever pieces of rock lay in its path.

"Oh! Oh!" she cried aloud. Suppose Martali had come down here. But she would be afraid. She would not go near this roaring brook.

Then Marta turned back toward the forest. Here also, Martali would be afraid. It was beginning to grow dark and all around not a human voice was to be heard; only the heavy roaring of the brook sounded ceaselessly through the stillness.

"Dear God, where would Martali go?" begged Marta, falling on her knees beside the stone which was wet with spray from the raging brook. She rested there a moment until the spray had cooled her face. Then she tried very hard to think what

Martali would do if she found this mountain torrent stretched across her path. Mightn't she walk along the edge of it rather than turn back into the dark forest? But suppose she slipped! Who would be there to help her if she fell in?

"Dear God, keep Martali safe!" she prayed again.

The prayer comforted her. She no longer felt as if she were walking alone, but as if the Spirit that lived in the blue fire over the glacier, in the dazzling flashes shot forth from the waterfall, in the enchanted garden, and in her heart also, were walking with her.

Now Marta followed the brook, climbing up the slippery rocks and down again on the other side, falling and sliding sometimes, but always catching on in time to save herself. At last she climbed down an especially steep ravine and, to her amazement, found herself standing in an open field. She ran on and on, still following the brook. The water bubbled along quite peacefully now and soon the sound of cowbells came to her ears. Why, she was in the pasture! She had found the way home, not meaning to find it at all. But she had not found Martali.

Meanwhile Peter, pale and worried, had returned to the chalet. He walked into the big room at the front—the room that served as kitchen, living-room and the twins' bedroom altogether—and found Heidi, her face tear-streaked, just putting a rebellious Tobi to bed.

"Oh!" she exclaimed, looking up at Peter whose torn clothing showed plainly that he had passed through many thorns. "Oh! You have not yet found her?"

"They are both lost now," he declared, his voice full of anguish. "Marta darted away before I could stop her. But now we will sound the Alp horn. If she hears it, she will think

Martali is found and come home. That is," he added, "if she has not lost the way."

So Peter brought out the long horn and, carrying it to the slope just above, placed one end on the ground and sounded its four solemn notes in a tune that was almost a cry:

"Ja, ho, li, ho!"

It echoed far beyond the pasture. The helpers, who were searching in the deep woods and as far away as the distant glacier, heard it and turned back, thinking Martali was found.

Marta was now at the far end of the upper pasture. It was here that Peter and Heidi used to come with the goats. First there would be a green slope; then above it, a rocky ledge covered with a soft red carpet of Alpine roses; then a rock again.

Under one of these rocks, the goats sometimes found shelter from the rain. Marta remembered following Tolpet there two summers before. She remembered also that there was a soft bed of moss inside this rocky cave. The Alp horn told her that Martali was found and now, realising how tired she was, she wanted nothing so much as to lie down and rest for a while. She wouldn't stay long; just long enough to stop this aching that she felt all over from so much climbing and searching.

She felt her way into the cave, as it had grown quite dark and she could no longer see. Now her hand rested on the mossy place and she lay down, full of weariness, with her head pillowed on her arm. The other arm was thrown out at her side . . . But this was not moss that she felt! It was fine cloth, such as little dresses are made of. But it couldn't be Martali's dress.

She must be dreaming. Someone had already blown the Alp
horn to announce that Martali was safe.

A faint sigh sounded, as though a child were just awakening
from a long sleep. Then Marta knew it was Martali and, in the
darkness, clasped her close in her arms.

"Oh," said the child, still drowsy. "I did find you."

"I found *you!*" exclaimed Marta, still hugging her.

"But *I* wasn't lost. Is it night now?" she asked, pulling herself
free of Marta's arms and looking about her. "Why did it get
dark?"

"The sun went to bed, dear. It's time you were home in bed
too."

"But this is my house," Martali protested. "I found it. I want
to stay here and sleep all night."

"You can't do that, dear. Come," coaxed Marta, taking her
hand.

"Why can't I stay?"

"Because you can't. Your mama will be worried. Come now,"
Marta repeated, beginning to grow impatient.

"But I don't want to go out in the dark! I don't want to go
out in the dark!" And, repeating the same thing over and over,
she began to kick and scream. Marta tried to carry her, but it
was no use. One little foot hit her over the eye and left a bruise
that stung and smarted.

"I'll take you pickaback," she offered. "Hold on tight! You
won't have to walk in the dark."

"But I don't want to go pickaback!"

"Well, what do you want?" asked Marta, exasperated.

"I want my mama!" screamed Martali. "I want my mama! I
want my mama!"

Suddenly Marta, who had seen so much all in one day, saw

something else. *She* was Martali. She was screaming aloud, "I want my grandma! I want my grandma!" while the echoes screamed all around in the lonely old château. She was her mama too. Now she knew how she must have frightened her mama; how worried and upset her poor papa must have been. The words came back to her. *Anything! Anything to get her off our hands!*

"What a child I must have been!" she exclaimed, speaking aloud.

"I want my mama——"

"Hush!" Marta commanded. "Stop your screaming and I'll take you to her. You should be glad you have a mama. You should be ashamed to run away like this. You're a bad little girl and you don't deserve the nice strawberries your mama brought home for you. You don't deserve such a good mama. And I don't either," Marta added, very low.

"I'm sorry," said Martali, and stopped screaming at once. The word "strawberries" worked like a charm. "I'll ride pickaback." And soon Marta felt the chubby little arms about her neck.

Now the moon had risen, full and bright. Everything shone in a mystic yellow light and the rocks in the pasture gleamed as white as pearls. The great snowfields beyond sparkled like pure silver as they climbed to the vast, star-studded sky. Guided by the lamp which Heidi had placed in the window of the chalet on the Alm, Marta struggled on with the child on her shoulders. But long before she had reached the house, she felt a pair of strong arms lifting her up and heard Peter's voice, saying thankfully to Heidi, "God be praised! Marta has found the child."

Chapter 20

The Departure

*M*arta had just finished composing a long letter to her mama. Now, as she read it over, she felt that there was still something she had left out. But, as she would soon be seeing her mama and papa, she could tell them the rest.

She was about to fold her letter, ready to post, when she remembered that she had never told Heidi exactly what she had decided.

"Heidi! Heidi!" she called. "Where are you? I want you to see my letter."

Heidi was in the cheese-room and had to dry her hands before she took the envelope, for she had just been washing the milk pails. Martali, anxious to make up for the worry she had caused, was standing on tiptoe to hang out strainers. Tobi was scouring away at the copper kettle and making faces at himself in the shining bottom while Peter turned and salted the cheeses.

"I'll have to find something to do to help Mama," Marta thought as Heidi took her letter.

On the Alm, July fifth.

Dear Mama:

I am coming home at the middle of this month so that we shall have six long weeks together before school begins. Then I shall come every Sunday. Nothing shall stop me. I have stayed away so long that now I must make up for it to you and Papa too.

Do not worry. You shall hear no more screaming from me. Martali was lost the other day and I found her, but at first she screamed so hard that I could hardly bring her home. It was just the way I used to do and now I know exactly how you must have felt after Grandma died and I kept screaming so hard and nothing could stop me. Anyway, I am thirteen years old—nearly fourteen and much too old for baby tantrums.

And, Mama, please don't stop entertaining. Jamy liked your friends and I know I shall too. But I do want just a little time to do very special things, such as walking around the lake and discovering all the beautiful places. Heidi said she learned to love the lake almost as much as she did the mountains and, if she could do it, I think I could too.

Perhaps this sounds like someone else writing you a letter and not the Marta you knew. You can blame it all on Heidi's enchanted garden. Some time when we come back to visit, and I do want to come back often, I would like to take both you and Papa high up to this beautiful garden on the edge of a glacier. Then you will see for yourselves why we call it enchanted.

While we were there Heidi explained about the cross and at last I understand why we are cousins and all about it. But I understand something else. It's about courage and so I am asking you, please let me travel all alone. I want to. You see, when a person has courage, all the things she used to be afraid of become big adventures, You will remember how I used to scream and cry and

*be afraid of trains. But you will see that they do not frighten me a
bit any more.*

*Another thing I used to be afraid of was meeting strange people.
But when I go to the school at Rosiaz I shall try and remember
that all the other new students feel just as strange as I do. Even
Heidi felt strange until Jamy and Lise and all the others spoke to
her and made her feel at home. She has told me so much about it
that I feel I know the school already and that it is up to me to
make other students feel at home and not worry about myself.*

*I'm very happy, looking ahead to all this. So do not be surprised
if your Marta bursts in on you any day now and bothers her
Mama and Papa for the rest of their lives.*

                                              With love,
                                              Marta

"Marta, this is a very brave letter," Heidi told her after she
had read it. "I'm proud of you, dearest. But then, a little girl
who can do what you did for Martali can do almost anything. I
think, dear child, you are about to make a great many people
very, very happy."

"I'm happy about it myself," Marta replied. "Now I remember so many things that I never thought of before. Everybody
says Lake Geneva is one of the most beautiful lakes in all the
world and, only a little way beyond it, the mountains are as
beautiful as they are here. You can see one of them in the
distance from our château."

"And from the school," Heidi put in, "you will be able to see
the Savoy Mountains, like low clouds, all along the horizon.
And they take you on trips—all the girls together. You learn
your history by seeing it. There are so many historic and
interesting places near Lausanne."

"And Papa says he has a boat! He told me about it last summer and said he would like to take me sailing. Now I can really go!"

And these joyous exclamations burst forth from Marta every few moments as she thought of something else. Each day her enthusiasm mounted until she could hardly wait to climb into the train that would take her to Vaud.

Finally the day of her departure came. Every kind of clothing lay about in such piles that there were no more chairs or benches left to sit on. Tobi and Martali, excited and eager to help, ran back and forth with their own and Heidi's things, causing still more confusion, as these articles only had to be put back in their places and the work of packing continued. But, little by little, everything disappeared into Marta's trunk and her two travelling bags.

One of Peter's helpers now lifted the trunk to his shoulders and started off with it. The travelling bags were piled on old Gaffer's back and Peter helped Marta to mount him. He would go with her, leading the horse down the steep path as far as the station in Maienfeld. There everything would be loaded into the train and she would continue her journey alone.

"I feel very high up," she announced as she found herself safely perched on the horse's back. The travelling bags were placed behind her as a kind of cushion and made her look nearly as queer as she felt.

"Are you really going?" asked Martali, watching the whole proceeding with wide eyes. Now the excitement was over and she had seen Marta mount the horse it came over her that it meant an end to their going to the pasture together.

"Yes, but I shall come back. Some day you will have to go away to school too, Martali."

"And Tobi too?"

"Yes, and Tobi too. Everybody has to go away some time. But you can always come back. Home is here."

"But you said you were going home to your mama and papa," spoke up Tobi, always practical.

"I think I now have two homes. Three," Marta added, "if you count the school."

"And four if you count the manor house. We must not forget to stop off and say good-bye to Mother and Chel and the Sesemanns," said Peter as he took hold of the bridle, ready to lead the horse.

"Remember me to your mama and papa, and to Jamy and Max when you see them," Heidi told her. "Oh, yes, and remember me to Monsieur Rochat if you take violin lessons at school. And if Miss Smith is still there, be sure and pronounce the *th* in her name. She is very particular about that. But I suppose there will all be new teachers," she added as though this were something sad.

"I'll love them whoever they are," Marta assured her. "Doesn't this look like a caravan, Heidi? I feel like a real discoverer. There should be flags flying and a band playing—but not the herdsman's song. That might make me homesick."

"You mustn't be homesick, Marta."

"I shan't be. I shall remember what you said—every word. I have the cross about my neck and always and always I shall remember 'Have Courage.' Indeed I shall."

"Good-bye, Marta! Come back soon!" called Tobi as they started.

"Good-bye, Marta! Good-bye, Marta!"

Martali's voice was a little tearful, but still she kept on calling. Marta smiled happily and waved her handkerchief.

She was still waving as the little procession moved farther and farther down the mountainside. The man with the travelling bags was ahead, but now the horse was catching up to him. The dot of white was Marta's handkerchief, still waving. "There should be flags flying," she had said. And this was her brave little flag. It waved until Heidi could no longer distinguish it. Martali was pulling at one side of her skirt and Tobi at the other.

"You still have us," Martali reminded her.

Now it was Heidi who had need of courage. Tears came to her eyes and, try as she would, she could not keep them back. For she knew that no matter how far away Marta travelled, she would always think of her as one of her children.

THE END